Beethoven's Encore
in the
21st Century

Also by C. C. Vaughan

FICTION

Sky Moon

CHILDREN'S FICTION

The Treasure of Longbearcd
The Girl Who Lived With Rabbits
Artie Goes to Hollywood

You-Draw-It Books:
Clyde, the Curly-Furred Mouse
The Girl Who Lived With Rabbits
The Tale of Artie's Tail
Artie Goes to Hollywood
There's a Pig in the Firehouse!
Badda-Badda's Bad Spells
The Horse Knows the Way, a Christmas Story
Magic Wiggle-Nose and the Dancing Christmas Trees
Dogfur

NOTE: Robert James Ellis has produced a companion CD of piano music for this book entitled *Beethoven's Encore in the 21st Century*. It is available separately.

Additional listening on YouTube.com of music mentioned in the book:
BumbleBee-thoven: youtube.com/watch?v=JzlqVwe_Dqc
Great Balls of Fire is in 2 parts on 2 different YouTube channels:
Pt. 1: youtube.com/watch?v=0-sE2lbCxKg
Pt. 2: youtube.com/watch?v=qQAI0RA4yaY

Beethoven's Encore in the 21st Century

C. C. Vaughan

Based on an Idea
by
Composer Robert James Ellis

CASTLEBROOK PUBLICATIONS

Beethoven's Encore in the 21st Century

Castlebrook Publications
1535 Farmers Lane, PMB 237
Santa Rosa, CA 95405
castlebrookbooks.com
youdrawitbooks.com
robertellis.name
e-mail castlebrookbooks@aol.com

Library of
Congress Control Number: 2015918612
ISBN 978-0692538319

This is a work of fiction. Names, characters, businesses, places, events and incidents are either the products of the author's imagination or used in a fictitious manner. Any resemblance to actual persons, living or dead, or actual events is purely coincidental.

Cover design by C. C. Vaughan
Cover and title page photograph by William Biehl
Interior book design by C. C. Vaughan

For my devoted and loving husband,
Robert James Ellis,
whose outstanding talent of composing
and of improvising on themes
by Beethoven
and other composers
inspired me to write this book

"To die, to sleep—To sleep, perchance to dream…"
William Shakespeare, Hamlet

I bought a journal today to record the events of my new life so people will know death is not the end. As some of the events have already occurred, I am not sure of the dates of them. Moreover, I often don't know the date, or don't want to bother finding out the date, so my journal will be more of a running account of events. Another thing I don't know about my new life here—

Is it a dream or is it reality, and does it matter which?

L. V. Beethoven

1

$\mathcal{M}$y life, that is this life now, began some time after my death in 1827. I don't know how long I slept. The only thing I remember was that I was walking with Wolfgang Mozart in a beautiful green meadow studded with fragrant white flowers. That was where I decided my future, for better or worse.

"Wolfgang, how long do you think I have been here?"

"It's timeless here, Ludwig, how can I tell?"

"Are we to remain here forever? The peace is getting to me. What can we do?"

"You can listen to heavenly music and wander the fields and woods. Hear the music?"

"Yes, but it's extremely boring. Who wrote it? I'd like to give them some lessons. I long for the passion of composing, and composing passionate music."

Mozart shrugged his shoulders. "We can compose if we so desire, but who will hear it? I haven't been able to find any paper and quills or I would write just for something interesting to do."

"Who can compose in this void with this mind-numbing serene angelic music constantly assaulting my ears? I almost wish I were deaf again so I wouldn't have to listen to it and could hear my own compositions in my head."

Mozart picked a flower and stuck it in a buttonhole of his vest. "I know what you're thinking, Ludwig, because I've thought it myself, but things have changed on Earth, and not for the better. I've heard from new arrivals that it's more tumultuous than ever. Bigger wars, more noise, more people, more police!"

"Good! I want to go back! I want to write my tenth symphony! That atmosphere should help me compose even more wild and passionate music than before."

"Ludwig, be careful what you wish for. It may come true, but not as you think. You can't just come back here any time you want. You have to live out a life until you are called back, or else kill yourself—and that's frowned upon. They might not let you back in."

"Perfect! What do I do, just wish to be there in Earth's present time and to write my tenth symphony?"

"Don't do it is my advice. I fear you will be driven mad—even more so than before."

"I won't be deaf, will I?"

"You would be better off deaf. I hear the noise is unbearable now, and the music a frightening cacophony. I prefer to stay here and enjoy the sounds of nature and," he smiled, "of my darling mistress Louisa."

"Well, Wolfgang, you stay here and enjoy your little dream. I'm going for the big reality. Something tells me I can compose my greatest symphony yet—my tenth—down there."

Mozart laughed raucously. "That something telling you is the Devil! I will pray for you, Ludwig. You will surely need it. I must warn you, don't tell anyone where you're from. They won't believe you and they might lock you up in an insane asylum."

"Don't worry. I won't. I may see you again sometime. Now I am going to make my wish come true."

"Wait! You have to take a valise with you." As he said that, a valise appeared, the handle in my hand. It was chained to my wrist!

"Clothes for my new life?"

"More than that," he said. "It *is* your new life. With the valise you will have the perfect life in which to write your tenth symphony. Don't lose it."

"How do you know that?"

"It's what I've been told. You will be called when it's time to return."

"Called? How will I know I'm being called back?"

"You'll know when it happens. I'll say no more, except to warn you—you can't sire children there."

"I've lived without children before, and I can do it again. I'm going there to write my tenth symphony. That will be my child." We shook hands and I took my leave of him. I walked on through the field, thinking of my desire and listening to my inner music over the so-called angelic music being perpetrated in that dull Elysium.

You may wonder why I am writing in English since I never mastered it in my previous life. The answer will become clear to you in a moment.

As Mozart had warned, the something telling me to return to Earth *was* the Devil. I had descended into hell—into the State of California! One minute I was ambling along in the green Elysian Field and the next minute I was in a quite different field, a football field! In the middle of a game, no less. At the time, I didn't know it was a game. I was confused. I didn't know what was going on. A monstrous voice akin to the description in the Holy Bible of God's thunderous voice was booming across the field.

"Who's that man? He just appeared out of nowhere on the field!"

Thousands of voices were screaming, surely caused by the agonies of hell. I tried to cover my ears with my hands to lessen the pain from the noise, but the valise got in the way.

Men in strange garments and shiny helmets were charging toward me. One of them threw something at me. It hit me on the head and I fell to the ground in a daze. I struggled to my feet and nearly tripped over the thing that hit me. It was an odd-shaped ball. Without thinking, I picked it up and ran the other way down the field, dodging the players left and right. I ran between a couple of posts at the end of the field. A wave of applause and cheering followed me. I kept running until I came to an open area away from the field.

You cannot imagine the terror I felt. I thought I was really in hell. *Have I been so sinful that God has banished me to this place?* I cried. I wailed, and then I looked at the rows and rows of large multicolored boxes with strange wheels. *What are those? Torture chambers of hell? Will they try to put me in one?* I was too exhausted to run but I walked as fast as I could down an open lane with arrows pointing to where I knew not.

Finally, I was out of that place. Suddenly, a terrible roaring noise and a great wind came from the sky. I looked up. A huge metal monster descended from above and landed in front of me. Two men in uniforms jumped down from it and accosted me. One of them handcuffed me. A metal box with flashing lights, some kind of coach I guessed, pulled up and two more men got out. They took me over to the coach, and made me lean against it, my back to them. One of them patted me over and took things out of my pockets. "What's in the briefcase?"

"I don't know. I never saw it before."

"Likely story. How could you never see it before if it's chained to your wrist?"

I dared not tell the truth. "I got hit on the head by a ball, and knocked to the ground. I was unconscious for a moment, and lost my memory."

"Are you a suicide bomber?"

"What? NO!"

"What's your name?"

"I don't remember."

He opened a wallet he had found in my pocket. "It says here your name is Van Bevin. Is that right?"

"If you say so."

He'd found a key as well, and unlocked the chain on my wrist.

"This case has combination locks. What's the combination?"

"I don't know what you're talking about."

The other man said to him, "Maybe it's a bomb. Set it down away from us. I'll call the bomb squad."

The first man looked at the case. "It's got writing on it. It says, "DANGER. Quantum field and particles. DO NOT OPEN."

The other man yelled, "Put it down NOW and get away!"

The first man said to me, "You're under arrest. You have the right to remain silent; anything you say can and will be used against you in a court of law. You have the right to speak to an attorney. If you cannot afford an attorney, one will be appointed for you. Do you understand these rights as they have been said to you?"

"Yes, but who are you?"

"I'm Police Officer Ryan." He shoved me into the back of the strange coach and shut the door. I tried to open it, but it was locked.

The police were arresting me, for what I didn't know. They waited for the bomb squad. After a few minutes two large coaches screaming like banshees pulled up. They were the bomb squad. One of the officers from the bomb squad opened the door and started questioning me. "What's in the briefcase?"

"I don't know. I got hit by a ball and fell down and hit my head. I've lost my memory of just about everything."

He got the contents to my pockets from Officer Ryan. "I have your passport here. Van Bevin, German citizen. What terrorist organization do you belong to?"

"None! I'm a musician, a composer."

"Why are you here?"

"To study your music and write a symphony."

"You talk like an American. Why's that?"

"Uh . . . my English teacher was American."

He said to the other men, "He's not saying much. Let's get the case x-rayed and see what's inside."

Officer Ryan and another officer got into the seats in front of me and started driving like demons down the road with their banshee horn blaring. I was scared out of my wits! *So this IS hell. I'm sorry, Father in Heaven. I don't know what I did to deserve this, but please forgive me and take me back to Heaven.*

They took me to the police station, stuck my thumb on a pad, stood me up against a wall, flashed blinding lights at me, then put me in a small room with a metal table and two chairs. I tried the door, but it wouldn't open. I sat down and pondered whether this was Earth or hell. So far, I'd been hit on the head, handcuffed, transported at breakneck speed and locked in a bare-walled room. What was that valise chained to my wrist? What were quantum fields and particles? How could a field fit in a small valise? I wished only to return to Elysium, but my wish was not granted. I was still in that room.

After a long while, Officer Ryan came in with the valise. "They x-rayed the briefcase and it was empty. There was some writing on the inside, though. It read . . . well, the first time it read, 'This is a dream. Wolfgang Amadè Mozart.' One of the officers wanted to x-ray it again because he couldn't believe it was signed Mozart. The second x-ray showed, "This is not a dream." Again signed by Mozart. Do you know anything about this?"

"No. Like I said, my memory is gone."

"Well, it doesn't appear dangerous, at any rate. You can have it back." He handed me the valise. I wasn't sure I wanted it, but I took it anyway.

"Here's your wallet and your other stuff. You're free to go." I stuffed the items in my pockets.

"Where will I go? I'm unfamiliar with this town and I have no transportation."

"We could give you a ride. Where do you want to go?"

"I could use a cup of strong coffee."

2

The police dropped me off at a strange coffeehouse called Starbucks. A few people were sitting outside at tables. They were staring at me. I suppose it looked odd that I had arrived in a police car. They were dressed strangely, the men in shirts with short sleeves and baggy short pants showing their bare legs. The women were dressed in less than the bawdiest harlots of my time. One young man had strange images painted all over his bare arms and legs. It was frightening. What had this world come to?

I went inside to see what I could get to drink. The aroma of fresh-ground coffee stirred in me a great desire for some. I preferred to make my own, but I had no means at the moment to do so. I had to settle for a cup from this coffeehouse.

There were shelves of odd-looking mugs and packets of coffee and tea. I sat down at an empty table and put the ball on one chair and the valise on another. I waited for a waiter, and waited, and waited. I grew impatient and yelled, "Where's the waiter?" I banged the table with my fist. *That hurt! I must remember to take care of my hands.* I want coffee!" Everyone in the place started laughing.

A young woman behind the bar replied, "Come up to the counter and I'll take your order."

With much agitation, and forgetting that customs may be different now, I bounded angrily up to the counter. The woman looked afraid. She asked in a very meek voice, "What can I get for you?" I was taken aback by her melodious female voice. I hadn't heard the voice of a woman in many years. She was young and pretty. She was wearing too much paint on her face and too few clothes. Judging from the other women I saw, it seemed to be the custom.

"Coffee."

"What size?" she asked.

"What size?" *How many sizes could there be?*

"Yes. Tall, Grande or Venti. Also, we have a new size, Trenta."

"Just a regular cup of coffee!"

"Light, bold, or decaf?"

"I don't know what you call them. Very strong!"

"You must want espresso."

"Italian? Okay, I'll try it."

"Single or double?"

I didn't know what she meant. I was exasperated by all these choices. "Both!"

"How about a pastry?"

I had to admit, even though I was impatient to drink, I was hungry as well. I looked at the strange pastries in the glass case. I couldn't decide. "Give me the one you think is the best."

"The brownie," she said. She took one out and put it in a small paper bag.

"Don't you have any plates?"

She got me a paper plate and put the bag on top of it. Then she pointed to the end of the counter. "Your coffee will be over there when it's ready."

I started over there when she said, "Can you pay for it now?"

Pay for it! I had forgotten about that part. I put down the plate and bag. I hoped there was some money in my clothes, but I had no idea. I started searching unfamiliar pockets. This was the first time I thought about my clothes. I didn't know what they looked like. At least I had long pants on. I didn't find any money in my pockets so I took out the wallet. Perhaps I would find some money in there.

Imagine my surprise when I opened it and saw a picture of myself at about thirty years of age! I looked more handsome than ever. The name under the picture was "Van Bevin," the name the police had called me. I also noticed I was five feet eleven inches tall! (Somehow I knew what the measurements meant, even though they were foreign.) *This must be Heaven, where I have shed my short sick old body for a new and improved one!*

"Well?"

I looked in all the compartments but found no money of any kind. What was I going to do? I pulled out a strange gold card and stared at it.

"We take cards." She held out her hand and I put the card in it. She did something with it and gave it back to me. *Is there no more money on Earth now, only cards?* "Do you want a receipt?"

"Of course," I replied. She gave it to me and I went over to get my coffee. It was in a cup made of thick paper, like all the others I saw around me. I took it and went back to my table.

Paper cups, paper bags, paper plates, and no waiters. Customs had definitely eroded since my death. At least the coffee and the brownie were good. I felt revitalized after consuming them. I took out my wallet to get a better look at my picture. I smiled to myself. *So this is how I look now? I'm a handsome devil.* I thumped the table with my hand "NO! No mention of the Devil!" I realized I had spoken those words—loudly. I looked up. People were staring at me. They must have thought me insane to be yelling to no one in particular.

I went back to studying my picture. A moment later I heard a feminine voice. "Do you mind if I sit here?"

I looked up. She was stunning. I stood up according to the custom of my time. My first thought was, *What is SHE doing here?* I felt I knew her. She looked like my Immortal Beloved, except for her dark hair. Was she? Did she know who I was? I was compelled to stare at her. She put her coffee on the table and sat down before I could respond with, "Please do."

As I sat back down, she looked me right in the eye. *Bold,* I thought. She had a silver-colored metal rectangular slab she set on the table. She pushed her long dark hair away from her face.

She opened up her silver slab. "What is that strange thing you have there?"

She laughed a little and her eyes pierced my soul.

"Seriously, I don't know what it is."

"Are you from another planet?"

"Not exactly." I had to come up with something plausible, or did I. She took my question as a joke, maybe I could tell the truth and she'd be pleasantly amused.

"I'm from Bonn, Germany."

"Surely they have notebooks in Bonn."

"Oh yes, but nothing like yours."

"You don't sound German. You sound more like an American."

"I studied English with an American. Of course we have notebooks there. Is that an American notebook?"

"Well, it's sold by an American company, but I imagine most of the parts are made in China."

"Parts?" I wondered just how many parts were in a notebook. Paper, binding, cover. I didn't know what to say to that.

She noticed the ball in the other chair. She picked it up. "Do you play football?"

"I did today, although I didn't mean to. I accidentally walked onto the field while I was ruminating. I got hit in the head with it. I blacked out briefly. I think I lost parts of my memory."

She put down the ball and reached for the valise. "What's in the briefcase?"

"Nothing, according to the police, except ambiguous messages from some composer. I don't remember why I have it. The police arrested me briefly while they examined it."

"It has writing on it. Let's see, 'Danger, do not open. Quantum field and particles.' Are you a physicist?"

"No."

She went on. "I never heard of anyone carrying around a quantum field in a briefcase. In fact, I haven't heard of anyone being able to put a quantum field in a briefcase."

"All I know is, the police x-rayed it, whatever that means. They said it was empty. It was probably a joke someone played on me."

She laughed. "I thought they might have found out whether the cat was dead or alive."

"What do you mean?"

"It's just a joke, based on Bohm's theory of quantum reality."

"Bohm? The police thought there was a bomb in it."

She laughed again. "It's not the same word. Spelled differently. Bohm was a physicist."

"They asked if I was a physicist."

"Anyway," she said, "I wouldn't open it if I were you, in case it's some new discovery. It could be dangerous, as the sign says. Maybe the case was lost by a physicist. He or she would be pretty upset that it's missing."

"Knowing I shouldn't open it makes me want to look inside." I picked it up and shook it a little. It made slight crackling and popping sounds.

"I don't think you should shake it, either," she warned. "Maybe you should put it in a safe deposit box at the bank so no one can steal it or open it."

"Nobody seems to know what it is or that I have it, so I don't think it matters where I put it."

"If you really have a quantum field in there, I have no idea what it could do. It does say 'danger.'"

I was tired of this line of conversation. I opened my wallet and showed her my picture. "I wonder if you could tell me where this address is. "I think I live there, but I don't remember where it is."

"It's a few miles away. I'll look up the directions for you." She opened her notebook.

"Look them up?"

"Yes."

"In your notebook?"

"Yeah." She laughed and shook her head. She started rattling off street after street, turn after turn.

"I'm afraid I can't grasp all that. I would take a cab if I had any money on me, but I don't."

At that moment I heard a startling sound! The first motive of my Fifth Symphony! *Da Da Da Dum. There it is again! Da Da Da Dum.* "My music!"

She looked a little startled when I said that. She took a small, narrow black box out of her bag. It happened again. It was coming from the black box. She pushed on the box with her finger and held it to her ear.

"Hi, Nick." She seemed to be listening. "Not tonight. I have to practice for a recital. I'll talk to you tomorrow. Love you. Bye."

Then she said to me, "You like Beethoven?"

"*Like* him? I *am* Beethoven!"

"That blow on the head must have done more than just daze you. It's given you a delusion."

I had to remember at all times that in my new life I was someone else. No one would believe I was Beethoven. "What I mean is, I'm a pianist and a composer. Like Herr

Beethoven I have composed nine symphonies and I'm ready to start on my tenth."

"Nine symphonies? Do you have copies? Can I hear them? Have they been played anywhere?"

"Yes . . . uh . . . in Germany. Small orchestras. I don't have copies with me."

"I'm a pianist, too, but I haven't written anything much. I play classical and romantic music mostly. I'm getting my Master's Degree in music at the university here."

"I'd love to hear you play," I said. "Do you play music of composers more modern than Beethoven?"

"Of course."

"Then I definitely want to hear you play. My memory is a little foggy, but I might have a piano at my house. My name is Van. What's yours?"

"Melanie."

"A beautiful name, Melanie. I'm interested in new music. I want to hear as much of it as possible."

"There's a recital of new compositions by students at tomorrow night. It might interest you."

I drummed my fingers impatiently on the table. "I can think of nothing worse than listening to students' feeble ideas of music!"

"I think they might surprise you."

"Like the football game?"

"No, not like the football game . . . I'm going to the recital. You can come with me if you want."

"That's a different story," I said. "I'd like to go with you. You can explain the music to me."

"Tomorrow night, meet me in front of Thompson Hall at six forty-five."

Melanie wrote something on a napkin and handed it to me. "Here's my phone number. Phone me if you decide not to go, because I don't want to stand around waiting."

"Phone?"

"Maybe you *have* lost your memory. The telephone, remember—transports sounds through wires or the air to a receiver? How are you getting home?"

"Cab, I guess. Can I get one on the street?"

"Not here. You'd have to phone for one. Do you have a cell phone?"

"I don't think so—not with me anyway. Money. I don't have any. Would they take my card?" I showed her my card.

"I don't know. Maybe not. I guess I could drive you if you promise not to try to seduce me," she said with a smile.

"I promise—not this time, anyway." I grinned a little sheepishly. She was quite lovely, and the thought of seducing her had been on my mind from the very beginning. I was not used to these passionate thoughts and feelings of the young. I wondered if I really looked thirty years old.

"How old do I look, Melanie?"

She looked at me thoughtfully. "I don't know. Thirty, maybe?"

Thirty years of age and I still have all my hearing! "We should get going. I have a lot to do after I drop you off."

I followed her out to an area where there were about twenty carriages. I had yet to see a single horse in this new world. She stopped at one of the carriages, opened a door, got in and shut it. I opened her door.

"The other side, Beethoven."

I went around and opened the door. It was small inside, but I managed to get in and sit down. I shut the door, and a low whirring sound commenced. She fastened a belt around herself.

"Put on your seatbelt." I fumbled with it until she took hold of it and fastened it for me.

Then the carriage backed up, then went forward, turned, turned again onto the busy street. I was scared out of my wits as she drove faster, other carriages whizzing by us in the opposite direction. I hid my face in my hands.

"Relax, Beethoven, you're safe with me."

I uncovered my face to look at her. "Your carriage goes so fast!"

"You'll get used to it. We call them cars, not carriages."

"Why are you calling me Beethoven?"

"I don't know. You kind of look like him, and you're from Germany, and you're a composer. It's a good nickname for you."

Then we rode up an incline onto a street with even more cars going even faster. She sped up until I yelled, "Slow down, you're going to kill us!" Shaking her head and chuckling, she slowed down a little. Soon we got off that street in hell to slower, tree-lined streets. Then we entered a narrow road thick with trees and other vegetation. It was beautiful! A few twists and turns and traveling up a hill, then she stopped the car.

"You're home," she said.

I looked out the window. It was a charming cottage with pale pink roses climbing the porch railing.

"Do you want to come in? See if I have a piano?"

"I don't have time today. Got your key?"

I searched my pockets and found a ring with three keys on it. "Maybe it's one of these."

"If you're having trouble with your memory, I think you should see a doctor. You might have had a serious concussion and bleeding in your brain."

I couldn't help laughing. "I don't believe it's that bad. My head doesn't hurt. It only hurt for a minute or two."

"If you want, I can give you a ride to the recital."

"That would be most appreciated."

"I'll pick you up at six-thirty tomorrow evening. Don't forget."

"I won't." I got out of the car and took my leave of her.

I was excited to be coming home to such a pleasant and quiet place nestled among the trees. I unlocked the door and went in.

3

The small entryway was open to a music room. I set the valise and the football on a table under the mirror in the entry and walked into the music room. An ebony grand piano about seven feet long greeted me. The name Bösendorfer was painted boldly on the side. *A German piano maker, though I have never heard of him.* I approached it with much excitement. Then I realized that first I needed to find a chamber pot. I didn't see one in my usual place under the piano. I didn't see one in the room at all.

I ventured into the hall and looked into room after room. A parlor with a couch and chairs . . . a big black window. I wondered briefly why anyone would want a black window, but I didn't stop to consider. I was looking for a chamber pot. *Kitchen . . . bedroom . . . closet . . . bedroom . . . bathroom!* *A room with a tub, a sink, and an open seat on top of a basin of water. Could this be a chamber pot of sorts?* It had a button on top. I pushed the button and the water went down a hole and more water came in. *This must be a modern chamber pot.* I tried it out, and it worked! This was a marvelous modern invention. Too bad it wasn't closer to the piano. I tried to move it but it was bolted to the floor.

I noticed some strange items on a counter with a basin. A small brush, a tube. I picked up the tube. "Toothpaste." A bottle that read "mouthwash." I assumed the brush was for my teeth. *I will try it later. Now, I only want to try the piano.*

Back to the music room I went. When I took a closer look at the piano, I saw a small portrait of myself painted on one side of the music rest. Then I saw the inside of the raised lid of the piano. Part of my hand-scored Sonata Number 14 was impressed somehow on the lid! I wasn't sure I liked these decorative touches. I was concerned it would be a distracting element when I was playing or working on a composition. However, I was pleased that the world had not forgotten me and had seen fit to memorialize me with a special piano. The keyboard looked a little longer than my piano in my old life. I counted seven octaves plus a minor third! *Wonderful! I can expand my writing, my improvising. I will give it a try.*

I sat down at the piano, "Ahh," I stretched and wiggled my fingers. It seemed to have been a very long time since I played. This time I would be able to hear what I played with ease! I thought I might as well start with my Sonata Number 14 since it was inscribed on the piano lid. I had only heard a piano in my mind for a long time. The reality was more heavenly than I remembered. The keys felt a little cold. I could tell they weren't ivory, but I couldn't imagine what they were made of. *A little distracting, but I will soon get used to it.*

I played effortlessly, then something came over me to change the music. I improvised on the themes for at least an hour. I felt so free in my new life, less inhibited. Oh, I know. I was not terribly inhibited in the last, but this freedom was lighter, more flowing. I played on and on, creating some incredible music. This piano was magical. I could easily coax the softest, most delicate tones from it or strong, powerful, massive tones at will. Truly, it was Heaven! *Mozart doesn't know what he's missing, or he would be here with me.* I promised myself I would tell him about it when I returned to Elysium. Maybe he would change his mind about returning to Earth.

After a while I felt exhausted and hungry. I got up and made my way to the kitchen. On the way out of the music room I noticed the valise and the football sitting on the table in the entry. I didn't want to be reminded of my frightful entry into this time, so I put them on the shelf in the entry closet. The valise made crackling sounds when I moved it. It was not the first time it had made that noise, but I did wonder how a seemingly empty valise could make such sounds. I was somewhat intrigued by this mysterious valise but, remembering Melanie's advice, I felt I dare not open it.

I closed the closet door and went into the kitchen. I had no cook to prepare my meal, so I opened the cupboard doors, one by one. There was nothing but strange boxes and sealed metal canisters. I found a loaf of bread in a paper bag on the counter. That was something, but not enough. I opened a tall silver-colored metal cabinet. It was cold inside. I found an opened bottle of wine, cheese, sliced ham, jars of preserves, grapes, tomatoes, lettuce, carrots, onions, and some other things I didn't recognize. They were all cold. I took out the wine, the grapes, the ham and the cheese, found a knife, and prepared myself a plate of food.

After my repast I tried the handles on the sink. Water came gushing out! Another amazing modern invention. Since I had no housekeeper, I washed off the dishes. While I was washing them, the water got very hot and nearly burned my hands. Hot running water! Another amazing invention. I went to see if the bathtub had hot running water and it did. I took a relaxing warm bath. By the time I finished, it was getting dark and chilly. I found some candles but found nothing to light them with or to start a fire in the fireplace with. *What kind of place has no flint and steel kit?*

It's dark, I might as well go to bed. The bed was incredibly comfortable and I quickly fell asleep. However, I did not sleep comfortably. First I heard Mozart laughing raucously at me as I ran down the football field. Then cars and football players were chasing me down the road. Melanie came into my dream and was laughing at me. She yelled, "You're insane!" Then she disappeared and I woke up. That was one thing I did *not* want her to think. I had to be careful how I behaved around her.

෴

Making coffee in the morning was a problem. I was storming around, throwing things because I didn't know how to prepare coffee in this world. I was pulling open drawers and spilling out the contents when I saw several leaflets. One of them read "electric coffee maker." The picture on the front matched an item on the counter.

"Aha!" I read the details. Next I looked for some coffee beans. I found a package, thank Heaven. I found a hand-operated coffee grinder on the counter. I counted out my sixty beans and ground them up. I put the coffee grounds as directed in the mesh basket, poured water into the tank, and pushed the "on" button. This was the best invention yet! In a few minutes I had my coffee. While I drank it, I perused the other leaflets.

I found instructions for the gas range. Cooking was done with a gas now. Supposedly I could turn a knob to make it flame. I tried it. It worked! This was very good, because I had no way to start a fire in the fireplace. I have never been much of a cook, but I could, and did, put some butter and eggs in a pan and scramble them. I ate them with some bread and apricot preserves. So, the necessities had been provided.

After breakfast I headed for the piano again. It was such bliss to play and hear myself! While I was playing, I heard something ringing. I thought it was my ears at first. I stopped and listened. It was coming from some contraption with a blinking light on the desk. I yelled, "Stop that noise!" I picked it up to throw it. The top part came off in my hand. I could hear a woman's voice. I put it to my ear. It was Melanie speaking from the top part. "Hello, hello! Beethoven? Are you there? Answer me."

"Yes! I am here! A phone! I didn't know!"

"You don't have to shout. Do you still want to come to the recital? I'll pick you up."

"Yes, I remember. Six-thirty."

I spent most of that day at the piano. In the afternoon I took a brief walk up the narrow country lane by my cottage. Beautiful trees, birds singing. Inspiring! A couple of cars drove by, and then about a dozen two-wheeled cars with riders on top—making a noise from hell. That ruined my enjoyment of nature. I yelled at them to stop their infernal noise. I'm sure they didn't hear me, but the yelling was a relief. I returned to the piano.

At six o'clock I started to get ready for Melanie. I washed my face and looked for a razor, but I couldn't find one. When I was at Starbucks, I had seen men with something like a day-old beard or even three days. Maybe it was the fashion. If so, I will fit in perfectly. I went to my closet and searched for something familiar to wear. I found a white shirt with buttons and an attached collar, trousers and a matching jacket. There were no vests. The clothes were strange, but I put up the collar on the shirt to feel a little more normal.

I was ready. I waited impatiently for her. I made up a love song, but I was so busy thinking of her while I played it that I couldn't remember it afterward.

4

*F*inally, I heard a knocking at the door. I opened it. There was Melanie—with a man! I had dreamt all day of an evening alone with her, talking, laughing, playing the piano together. Who knows what else might have transpired. My dream shattered, I glared at him, a tall thin man. He looked a little like a crane. He hadn't shaved, either. He smiled and stuck out his hand, which I grudgingly shook. I did not smile. How could I?

"Hi, I'm Nick," he said.

I let go of his hand and took Melanie's, which I kissed in the best French style. She pulled her hand away rather abruptly. "Nick wanted to come along to the recital. If you're ready, we'd better get going."

Nick went to the driver's side of the car and got in, Melanie took the front seat next to him. That left me to sit in the back alone. My mind was racing. *I must find a way to get close to her.*

We arrived just in time for the performance. The university theater was not large and there were only about forty people in the audience. Melanie went first to a seat and Nick followed her. I practically climbed over them to sit on the other side of her. "This way you can explain any music to me that I don't understand."

The horrible music that followed I cannot describe, except to say melody and scale were not in the students' vocabulary. The worst non-music I had ever heard! It was far worse than I had expected of any student. Maybe this was hell after all. At the intermission we got up. As we walked out to the lobby, Nick held Melanie's hand in his! Things were not going the way I had hoped. Obviously she was his. I wanted her to be mine. How could I win her?

"Well, Beethoven," she said, "what did you think of the music?"

"Music? It is *not* music! I would like to show them what music is!"

"You can't do that. This is their recital. You can't just take it over."

I saw coffee and pastries. "Does anyone want coffee?" They followed me to the refreshment table. Melanie asked if I had gotten some cash.

"Cash?"

"Money."

"No. I don't know where to get it."

Melanie paid for my coffee. She said, "If you don't know your PIN number, you can write a check at your bank."

PIN number? The checks, as least, I understand. Maybe there are checks at my cottage.

"You'll have to explain PIN number to me later."

We engaged in small talk for a few minutes. Nick was doing most of the talking about his scientific theories about which I understood nothing. Then we returned to our seats. I would have left the theater, but I didn't know how to get home—and I didn't want to leave Melanie.

After the final ridiculous performance, we went out to the car. I asked Melanie if she wanted to come to my cottage and play my Beethoven Edition Bösendorfer grand piano. She was excited at the thought of playing such a marvelous instrument. Nick, though, didn't think it was a good idea. He said, "I can't go. I have to grade exam papers. Melanie, don't you have some practicing to do?"

"If you were a pianist, you'd understand why I have play that piano. That will be practicing enough." She kissed him lightly and got in the car. We dropped him off at his apartment.

At last, I was alone with Melanie! She drove us to my cottage. I fumbled with the key in the dark. Suddenly a light was shining on the keyhole. Melanie had a light! A flashlight, she called it. We went in. She touched something on the wall, then there was light in the house!

"What did you just do?"

"I turned on the light. Now I'll turn on the heat. It's cold in here." She fiddled with a little rectangular box on the wall.

"That little box turns on heat?"

She gave me a look I didn't understand. Skepticism? Impatience? It was something I should have known if I were from this century.

"I want to find my checks before I hear you play." I remembered seeing a desk in the music room. I found the checks in the desk, in a little book with a check register. I showed Melanie the checkbook and asked, "Is 1,827,000 a good amount to have in the bank?"

She was walking around the piano, inspecting it. "Yeah, it's a lot of money."

"That's odd," I said. "The amount's the year I . . . uh . . . Beethoven died," I said.

"Eighteen twenty-seven *is* the year Beethoven died. Did you do that on purpose?"

"What?"

"Have 1827 in your account."

"No, I had no idea. I have just one more thing to ask you before you play the piano. Something in the kitchen."

She followed me in there. I opened the top part of the big silver cabinet. "What do I do with these boxes of frozen food?"

She took a box out and showed me how to read the instructions. She showed me the microwave and how to push the buttons. Another amazing invention!

"You don't remember anything! I really should make you an appointment with a doctor about your head injury."

"There's nothing wrong. I had a cook and housekeeper in Germany. I had no need to know about domestic matters. What I do need is a ride to the bank. Once I have cash I can use cabs."

"I noticed you have a garage. Maybe there's a car in there?"

"I don't think so."

"You don't think so? Have you forgotten?"

I thought I might as well be truthful, because if I said no and there was one, she'd know I'd forgotten anyway.

"Yes, I don't remember."

She headed for the door. "Let's go look."

The patio lit up as we went out. This generation likes to light up everything, night or day. I followed her to an outbuilding.

She opened the door and found a light switch.

"You forgot you had a Mercedes?"

"What's that?"

"A very expensive German car."

I laughed. "Of course. Now I remember. I would have a German car, wouldn't I."

It may seem that getting hit on the head on a football field is a less than perfect start to my new life, however, it gave me a perfect reason why I had no memories of a life before that—a reason people would believe. Any ignorance of people, places, and objects could be attributed to my memory loss.

"I don't remember how to drive. I could pay you to drive me to the bank in it. I could pay you to be my driver."

"I could use the money, but I can only drive you when I'm not busy with school. I'm not sure Nick will like the idea."

"Does he tell you what to do?"

"He tries to sometimes, but I rarely listen. Maybe I just won't mention it to him."

"Is he your husband?"

"No, my boyfriend."

"Is that like a lover?"

She smiled. "Yes, like a lover. I don't think I'm very serious about him. I'm not ready to get married, but if I were, I'm not sure I would choose him."

"I can see why not. Vapid. Uninteresting."

She attempted to defend him. "He's not vapid or uninteresting. He's a physicist, quiet, soft spoken."

"What a recommendation for a passionate relationship!"

She gave me a long look. I couldn't tell if she was annoyed or if I'd raised a bit of passion in her.

"Tomorrow I would like to go to the bank and a food market. Would you be my cook, too? I'd pay you extra for that."

"I'm afraid I don't have enough time for cooking. Maybe once in a while."

"Whatever you can do would be greatly appreciated."

"Let's go back to the house. I want to play your piano."

"And I want to hear you play it."

We returned to the cottage and she sat down at the piano. "What would you like to hear?"

"Uh . . . anything you like."

"How about a Chopin nocturne?"

"Sounds good." What else could I say? I had never heard of the man. I hoped he was better than the students I had heard. "When was he born?"

"Eighteen-ten."

This might be good music since he lived close to my time. It will be interesting to hear.

She began to play. I soon felt dragged down to the sorrows and gloom of night.

"That was lovely, Melanie. Such sensitivity. The music —the sounds of the night, the lovemaking, the sighing, the crying."

"Very astute of you," she replied.

"I should hope so. I've been a musician most of my life. No one knows better than I the sounds of love and sorrow that come upon us in the dark and quiet night."

"Did you lose someone you loved?"

"She was never really mine to lose. She was married to another. We had only a few nights of love, and the rest—sorrow."

"You'll love again."

"Perhaps, but will it be any better?"

She smiled, that radiant, glowing smile. "Sometimes you have to work hard to love better."

"I put so much work into my music that I don't know if I would have much left to work on love. Play something else. What other composers do you like?"

"Debussy. *Ce qu'a ve le vent d'Ouest*. What the West Wind Saw."

"A French composer."

"Yes." She began. It was the most disconnected piece of music I had ever heard. At first I thought it was a ridiculous piece of bombastic drivel. As I listened, though, and thought of the title, yes, wind could act like this. Quiet one moment, roughly scattering leaves the next. Perhaps a good musical interpretation of the event. However, I think music should express more important things—the emotions of people in good times and bad. Love, passion, happiness, sorrow, death, even war. I said as much to Melanie.

"Nature is just as important, if not more so, the way humans are destroying the environment and natural habitats of wild animals."

"Natural habitats? Uh . . . yes, of course. It's a strong, masculine piece for a woman to play. I would think a woman would play more gentle music."

"I play all kinds of music. A good musician, male or female, is not bound by 'feminine' or 'masculine' labeling of music. We all have feminine and masculine essences, even you."

"Do you play Beethoven?"

"Of course."

"Play some Beethoven for me."

"You're so into Beethoven and probably play him so well, I wouldn't feel confident. I'd be nervous and make mistakes. It's your turn, Beethoven. You play Beethoven for me."

"Not today. I don't want to spoil the delicate and sensitive mood your music has created in me. Next time I will play for you."

"Well, then, I'd better go. Studying to do." She moved toward the door but I got there ahead of her and opened it. I was thinking of taking hold of her and kissing her passionately, but before I could act, she brushed my cheek with her lips, turned and walked out the door. I stood there watching until she drove off.

5

Melanie was to pick me up at ten in the morning. I awoke at five, so it was going to be a long wait. After a breakfast of eggs and ham, I got dressed in anticipation of her arrival. There were still hours to go before she would arrive, so I looked around for paper to write music on. I had an idea for one of the movements of my new symphony. I searched in the desk. I found some manuscript paper in the desk drawer. I also found some music sketchbooks. Then I needed quills and ink. I looked everywhere and could not find a quill! What kind of place has paper and no quills?

I looked again. There was a jar on the desk with sticks of various kinds in it. I pulled one out. It was yellow with a sharp gray point—a pencil. There were also colored pencils which I occasionally like to use. I pulled out a black stick. A little point was sticking out at the bottom. It looked like the instrument Melanie had used in the coffeehouse. I might as well try it. There it was—black ink! A little awkward to use, not like a quill. I had been provided with so many things here, why not quills and ink? Well, I wasn't provided with a housekeeper, either, so I had to live with the way things are now. I couldn't find anything with brown ink, which I preferred for drafts. I would have to use the new-fashioned pen with black ink. Then I wondered what year it was. I looked around for evidence of the year, but couldn't find anything with a date on it.

The date was really of no use at the moment, so I began sketching a love theme that was playing in my mind. I planned to include it in my symphony. Maybe I would dedicate the whole symphony to Melanie, but this would probably be the only part inspired by her, or would it be? I played around with it on the piano for a while, then felt inspired to score half the movement! I liked it, but wondered how long it would be before the other movements would come to me. I had seen little of this world so far, and I wanted my experiences to be imbedded in the symphony. It was going to take awhile, a year or two perhaps.

After a while I was interrupted by a knocking at the door. I was so engrossed in writing that I had forgotten about going anywhere, about where in time I was; I'd even forgotten about Melanie.

I angrily stomped to the door and flung it open. "What do *you* want! Oh, Melanie, sorry. I was in the middle of writing and forgot where I was."

She gave me that bold stare again. "Well, are you ready?"

"Yes."

She stared at my head. "You might want to comb your hair first. You look like a wild man." I turned to look in the mirror on the wall. Indeed I did look wild. I ran my fingers through my hair until it calmed down.

I turned back to her. "Better?"

She smiled. "Much. Do you have your checkbook?"

"Oh." I went and got my checkbook out of the desk.

I dreaded getting in her car again and speeding down the road, but at least I was prepared for it this time. I restrained myself from covering my eyes the whole trip, but it wasn't easy. I admonished her several times to slow down, to no avail.

Finally, we arrived at the bank. She suggested I write the check for five hundred dollars so I wouldn't have to come back too soon.

"What is the date, my dear?"

"It's right in front of you."

"This? 2015?" She nodded. "**2015!**" I shouted it so loud everyone stared at me. They looked alarmed.

"Keep your voice down, Van. You don't want to act suspicious in a bank."

I mulled over the year, 2015, as I took the check to the clerk, who looked at my check. "L. V. Beethoven? Let me see your driver's license." I took it out and showed it to her.

"Your license says Van Bevin."

I laughed. "Sorry, I'm a composer. Beethoven's my favorite. Absent-minded of me." I stuffed the check in my pocket and wrote out another one. *How long is it going to take me to remember my new name?* That done, I returned to Melanie.

"Did you find your PIN?"

"My pen? I used the bank's pen."

She seem exasperated. "No! Your *bank* PIN, P-I-N!" She grabbed my checkbook and found the PIN in the back of the checkbook — "Beethoven10." She laughed at that. "You are really obsessed with him!"

I wanted to say I *was* him but that might be the last time I would see her. She showed me how to use the ATM machine. I got a hundred out. Another marvelous invention!

"Is there any shopping you want to do?"

"I don't know." I said. "What should I buy?"

She rolled her eyes.

I thought a moment. "Oh, I know. Some bread and cheese, and perhaps a cake. I would also like a notebook. I want to keep a journal of my experiences."

I won't go into the description of the supermarket; I'm sure you already know what it's like. Suffice it to say I felt I was in a fantastical dream. Maybe I was. Maybe this life is just a dream. If so, I have quite an imagination. Rows and rows and rows of everything under the sun, most of which did not exist in my past, and most of which I knew nothing about. The entire time I was trying to look at things, some horrible so-called music was blaring all over the store. I was soon so confused I just handed Melanie some money and frantically ran up and down the aisles until I found a door out of there. Melanie gathered the needed items and met me outside.

We went back to the cottage and Melanie came in with me. She fixed us lunch. We had a pleasant meal, then I watched her put the dirty dishes into a black lower cabinet in the kitchen. "So this is what you do with dirty dishes? Just hide them in a cabinet?"

She laughed. "It's an automatic dishwasher. You put the dish powder in here, close it up and push this button."

"Another amazing invention!"

"You really don't know anything, do you?"

"Like I said, I used to have a cook and housekeeper. I don't know what she did with the dishes."

"Now I have to go."

"When will you come back and fix us a dinner?"

"I can come on Wednesday at six."

"Very good, my dear Melanie. I can hardly wait until you return."

She smiled her sweet glowing smile and left.

6

It seemed to take forever for Wednesday at six to arrive. In reality it was two days before Melanie knocked on my door. She had a bag of groceries which I took from her and carried into the kitchen. She fixed a marvelous Italian dish of spaghetti and a salad. We also had bread and red wine. For dessert, we had cake and champagne.

After dinner I was ready to play something for her. "I like to improvise. I will improvise on my fifth symphony." I hadn't played more than four notes before she interrupted.

"That's *Beethoven's* fifth, not yours!"

"Heh, heh," I laughed feebly. "Just joking. I like to improvise on Beethoven. I feel his spirit guiding me."

"Go on."

I went on, and on, and on, exploring so many tangents of the themes. I must say, though it may brand me a braggart, that I played fabulously, far better than I ever had before. This stormy piano with dark tones aided me in my fanciful flight from my written music. When I was finished, I asked her what she thought.

"I'm speechless. Well, no, I can say, you are absolutely the most brilliant improviser I have ever heard!"

"Have I captivated you?"

"Captivated?" She appeared to be considering something. "You have scrambled my brain. I feel a little dizzy."

"Good," I said with a smile. She was standing near me, so it was easy to move a step closer and put my arms around her and kiss her. She did not resist. We wound up in the bedroom and the most passionate lovemaking ensued.

Afterwards, she said, "I don't know what came over me. I feel hypnotized by you."

"I'm glad, because I love you, my darling Melanie. I feel I've known you for centuries. Do you remember when we were together about two hundred years ago?"

She laughed a sweet little laugh. "No, but I do feel I've known you forever. I'm not sure I want to love you. I think you're strange, but I can't seem to help myself."

"Our love," I said, "was ordained in Heaven. One must not fight what was ordained in Heaven, but surrender as I have." I caressed her hair, kissed her gently.

She moved to get up. "I have to go. I have an early class in the morning."

I don't like to go into details of lovemaking. I find it crass and vulgar to speak of it to the general public. However, I will mention a one-word invention that I completely dislike, and it almost ruined our evening together—condom.

Afterwards, she said if I would get tested for AIDS, I wouldn't have to use one. "What is AIDS?"

"A deadly disease."

"What's the test?"

"They take some of your blood and test it."

"Oh my God, they take my blood! I won't let them!"

"Just a little bit. You won't miss it."

There wasn't much I wouldn't do for Melanie. This was just the first of many unpleasant tasks she would require of me.

෨

I was pleasantly surprised the next afternoon when Melanie showed up at my door with a bag of groceries for an evening meal. "I have some extra time today," she said. She took them into the kitchen and I followed her.

"I was wondering how I can learn more about the world. Maybe it would help my memory."

"Well, we could try your TV. You have a big screen in the den."

"The den?"

She sighed and led the way. "Here," she said. She sat down on the couch and picked up something like a cell phone. She pushed a button on it. I sat down next to her.

Suddenly, the black window lit up with figures of men in helmets and bayonets on their rifles.

I leapt up from the couch. "Come on, Melanie! They'll kill us! Let's get out of here!"

"Funny," she said.

"Come on," I implored.

"I'm not going anywhere." She seemed unperturbed by these strange soldiers outside the window.

I couldn't leave her there alone in such danger. I took hold of her and tried to drag her out.

"Take your hands off me!" She roughly pushed me away and continued watching. I stood behind the couch and watched. The men were talking. Then there were explosions in a field with men running, falling, flying through the air. Flying machines dropping bombs. Then huge metal wagons with cannons on top started rolling towards us, then turned toward a village. Then some other wagons came from another direction and demolished those wagons with their cannons.

People came running out of their homes in the village, cheering and waving cloths at the new wagons which had apparently vanquished the enemy.

Melanie turned to me. "You're white as a sheet and shaking! It's only a movie about World War II. It's not real. Have you been in battle? Do you suffer from shell shock?"

"Movie?"

"Moving pictures! Not real!"

"So there wasn't a war?"

"Oh, there was a war, all right—a lot of wars. This was a screenplay about a real war."

"Oh, a play. How does it get into my home?"

"Television. Like a phone receives sound transmissions, a TV receives visual and sound transmissions. Van, you are going to have to go to a doctor about your head injury or I can't continue our relationship. You've forgotten far too much."

"I don't have a head injury! I refuse to go to a doctor. What can he do?"

"I don't care what you think about it. I insist you go to a doctor if you want to continue seeing me."

That did it. I had no choice. I would have to go to a doctor. He would find out my head was not injured and she would be satisfied. "All right. I will go to a doctor."

"After that, I'm going to arrange for you to give a concert at the school. Everyone should hear you play. You're totally amazing. We'll record it and get you on tour."

"I would like nothing better, except being with you."

7

We were sitting in the doctor's waiting room with a few other people. I filled out some forms, then I looked around the room. One man had a large bandage around his head. I wondered what had happened to him. Had the doctor cut his head open? Would he want to cut mine open? I wasn't going to let him! The other people seemed normal. They were reading papers. I saw some papers on the table next to me. One said "TIME" on it. *How appropriate for my situation. Maybe I will learn something if I read it.* I picked it up. On the cover was a picture of a bloody sword and the words, "Will the Beheadings Ever End?" I thought the French Revolution had long been over. I threw it back on the table. I didn't want to think of my head being cut off. For all I knew, in this century they cut off defective heads and put on new ones.

I leaned over to Melanie. "It's taking too long. Let's go."

"We've only been here five minutes. You can wait a little longer. Read a magazine or something."

"I already tried that. It was frightening."

"Van Bevin," a woman called. I didn't respond because I forgot that was my new name. Melanie nudged me.

"That's you. Let's go."

We were ushered into a small room with a couple of chairs and a bed of sorts. The woman wanted me to sit in a particular chair. Then she put a band around my arm. "What's this?"

"I'm just taking your blood pressure."

"I want to keep my blood," I said and pulled off the band.

She snickered. "I'm not removing your blood. Just measuring how well it's pumping through your veins. It won't hurt."

"Okay, then." I let her put the band back on. She pumped a little ball in her hand. The band felt tight, but it didn't hurt. Then she ran some little gadget lightly around the front of my head. That didn't hurt either. After that, she said, "Doctor Roberts will be with you shortly," and left the room.

After a few minutes Doctor Roberts came in. He shook my hand. "So you got hit on the head with a football and fell down. Did you black out?"

"No, but I felt dazed. It only lasted a few seconds."

"Where exactly did the ball hit you?"

"Here, on the left side."

"Did you hit your head when you fell?"

"I don't remember. I lost some of my memory." I wasn't about to tell him I was Beethoven returned to Earth from Elysium and hadn't lost any memory at all.

"Your case doesn't sound too serious. Memory lost like that usually returns within a short time. Just to be on the safe side, though, I want you to have an MRI."

"Are you going to cut my head open?"

The doctor laughed. "No, I'm not going to cut your head open. Magnetic Resonance Imaging. You haven't heard of it?"

"If I did, I've forgotten it. Does it hurt?"

"Not at all, but it's noisy."

"That won't bother me. I'm used to noise." *More noise. Everything is noisy now.*

He gave me a paper to read about MRI. Don't wear this or that. Don't move. Wear headphones because it's very loud, and so on. After I read it, I was taken to another room and asked if I wanted headphones to listen to music while they scanned me because the machine was noisy. I was afraid the music would be horrid and preferred plain noise to it. Then I was told to lie down in front of the machine so they could scan my brain! *What I go through for love, for Melanie.* They promised it wouldn't hurt so I said to go ahead.

The noise was horrible. I let out a yell and tried to get my head out of there. It to took some doing to calm me down.

"Have you got Beethoven's Fifth Symphony on headphones?" He did, and gave me the headphones. I was able to increase the volume to drown out most of the noise, but I thought I could feel the magnetism altering my brain. I didn't like it at all.

Dr. Roberts found nothing wrong with my brain. He suggested I see a therapist to help with my memory problem. Unfortunately, Melanie heard him say that.

"I think you *should* see a therapist," she said. "You need help getting your memory back."

"It will come back on its own. He said so."

"How about a hypnotherapist who could also help with your Beethoven obsession?"

I yelled at her. "I don't have a Beethoven obsession, and if I did, it would only be helpful for a composer!"

"Don't yell in the doctor's office."

I lowered my voice just a little. "I don't think you will listen otherwise!"

Melanie hurried out the door. When we were in the car and I had calmed down, I asked her, "What is a hypnotherapist?"

"They use hypnotism to bring to light repressed memories. Maybe it will help you remember. I know a woman who does that."

"What is hypnotism?"

"She'll relax you and bring your mind to a focused level and hopefully any repressed memories can surface."

"Sounds like Mesmer! That charlatan! Animal magnetism indeed! I'll have none of it!"

She was shaking her head slightly. "It's not mesmerism and if you don't at least try, I'm not going to see you any more."

That did it. I didn't think I could live without her. My chance for Heaven on Earth would be snatched away in an instant. *Really,* I told myself, *all I have to do is talk to the hypno woman awhile and Melanie will see it won't work.*

8

The next day we went to see the hypnotist. Her name was Lorraine. She asked if she could record our session. I thought she wanted to make notes, so I agreed. All she wanted was to get me to close my eyes and relax. It wasn't easy at first, but I did gradually relax. I may have even gone to sleep. I don't remember.

Afterwards she studied my face for a moment and asked me if I remembered any of our session. I only remembered closing my eyes and relaxing.

Then she turned on a movie on a small screen. It was Lorraine and I on the screen! "What am I doing there?"

"You said I could record our session."

"I didn't know you were going to put me on television. Can anyone else see that?"

"No."

On the screen Lorraine asked, "What year is it?"

I started speaking in German.

"English, please. Speak English."

In German I said I didn't speak English well.

She stopped the movie. "That's all for today. I have to find an interpreter before we can have another session.

When I find one, I'll give Melanie a call." I was glad that was over, at least for the time being.

Melanie was too busy to see me for the next two days. I worked on the "Melanie" movement of my new symphony. I microwaved frozen dinners, drank coffee and ate cake, and played the piano.

On the third day I got a call from Melanie. Lorraine had called and said she found an interpreter. We went to so see her at three o'clock that afternoon. I was introduced to a young man named Ernst, a college student from Munich who was studying music.

"Ernst, you must agree not tell anyone what you hear," I said.

"Of course not. It's confidential. By the way, I attended your concert. You were amazing. It was almost as if Beethoven were on the stage improvising on his own music! I wish I could play like that."

"Thank you for the compliment. I often feel that I *am* Beethoven when improvising on his music."

"Let's get started," Lorraine said, and she began the relaxation routine.

"Well, Lorraine, when are you going to hypnotize me?"

Lorraine laughed a little. "We're all done."

"I don't remember anything. What happened?"

"Do you want to watch the video?"

"The what?"

"The TV, the movie."

"The video. Sure."

So we watched the video. I spoke German during most of the session. Here I will translate it into English.

Lorraine:	What is your name?
Me:	Ludwig van Beethoven.
Lorraine:	Isn't it Van Bevin?
Me:	No!
Lorraine:	What year is it?
Me:	1826! (I was yelling.) You know the year, and who I am! Why bother me with such stupid questions?
Lorraine:	Are you ill?
Me:	Yes! Again a stupid question! I am always ill! I just want to rest! Leave me alone!
Lorraine:	Let's go forward in time to 1990. What is happening in 1990?
Me:	(I calmed down here.) I don't know. I'm dead. I'm in Elysium. Green fields, flowers, doing nothing.
Lorraine:	Let's go forward in time a little more.
Me:	There is no time here.
Lorraine:	Is there anyone else there, in Elysium? Have you talked to anyone?
Me:	Wolfgang.
Lorraine:	Wolfgang who?
Me:	Wolfgang Mozart. A courageous composer but spineless when it comes to the real adventure of returning to Earth.
Lorraine:	Returning to Earth?
Me:	Yes.
Lorraine:	Have you returned to Earth?
Me:	(Now I was speaking English.) Yes, I have.
Lorraine:	When was that?

Me:	2015. I don't know the day or month.
Lorraine:	How did you come to Earth?"
Me:	I don't know. Just wished it. I wished to write my tenth symphony. Didn't have time before. Mozart gave me a valise to aid me in my wish. I was walking in an Elysian field and suddenly I was walking on a football field. I got hit by a football. I will say no more!

Lorraine woke me and the video ended. Melanie looked perplexed. Lorraine didn't say anything for a minute. Then she asked me, "Are you sure you were hypnotized?"

"Yes, I must have been because I remember nothing."

"Do you have multiple personality disorder?"

"I don't know what that is, but I don't have it."

She then wrote a check and gave it to Ernst. He said, "Thanks, Lorraine. School is expensive. I can sure use this. I must tell you before I go that Van seemed to be speaking an old-fashioned German. It is not very modern."

"Thank you, Ernst. I'll make a note of it."

When Ernst had gone, Lorraine said, "It will take me some time to analyze the video and do some research. I'll contact Melanie when I'm finished."

In the car, after a long silence, Melanie said, "I don't know what to think about your session. It was very weird. Were you really hypnotized or did you make it all up?"

"I really remember nothing of what I said."

"Your delusion seems to run deep."

"It's not a delusion! Maybe I was just having a dream!" How could I convince her it was not a delusion? I didn't believe I could convince her it was the truth that I was Beethoven returned to Earth on a football field. Maybe I could get her to believe something else.

"Do you believe in reincarnation?"

"I don't know," she said. "It could be one explanation but I don't want to think about it any more. I'm going to drop you off and go home. I'm very tired." She got out a small piece of paper and handed it to me. "Here's the phone number to call a cab if you need one. I've been meaning to give it to you, but didn't get around to it until now."

I called her a few times after that, but only got her voice mail, so I dove into my music until I could see her again.

9

*I*t was the day of my concert and I still hadn't heard from Melanie. I guessed I was on my own. I called the cab company and arranged for a cab to pick me up at six-thirty.

I got dressed in a white shirt with little ruffles, a black jacket with shiny black lapels and black trousers. Then, as it was nearly six-thirty, I waited on the porch for the cab.

This being the twenty-first century, the cab was of course horseless. I got in the back seat. Horrible, deafening music was playing in the cab. I had to shout over it to be heard. "Stop that noise!"

"You don't like music?"

"I love music, but not that noise!" The cab driver stopped the noise and we rode in silence. His driving was even more frightening than Melanie's. Thank God I arrived in one piece.

There wasn't time to check the piano. A stage hand showed me to a dressing room where I could relax. I couldn't relax, though. I paced back and forth in the dressing room with some excitement, running through the music in my mind and how I was going to improvise on each piece. I knew my mental ideas would only be roughly followed. Inspiration of the moment would take hold and I knew not where it would take me.

Finally, I was called. I saw from the wings that Melanie was introducing me! As she left the stage, she gave me her sweet smile. My spirit soared. *This will be a great performance!* I entered the stage and bowed to the audience. I received a polite applause. I surveyed the audience. They seemed to be a mix of students and teachers. I took a moment to walk around the ebony grand piano. *It must be nine feet long! This will be quite enjoyable.* I sat down and prepared myself for a moment. I would improvise first on a light tune by Mozart. It would relax the audience and hypnotize them with my flights of fancy.

This Yamaha piano had a lighter sound and feel than my Bösendorfer, but it was quite delightful for the Mozart. I wove so many new notes around Mozart's themes, I wondered what he would have to say about it if he knew. I wished he were here to hear it. I thought he would like what I did. I could almost hear him laughing in amazement. The audience liked it well enough and gave me a hearty applause. I played one more Mozart improvisation with a little more gusto and the audience seemed to like it even more than the first.

After that I got into my own works. I must have spent twenty minutes or so on the first one. The applause and bravos were more resounding than I had gotten for the Mozart. After that there was a little intermission and I went back to my dressing room. I didn't want to be inundated with people and questions when I still had more to play. I was immensely pleased with my performance so far. I had never improvised so well in my life, new or old! New harmonies were coming in—such inspiration I had never received in my old life. It was magical!

There was a knock at my door, and then it opened. It was Melanie! "That was wonderful, Van! The crowd loved it."

I drew her into the room and hugged her. "I'm happy they did, and I'm so happy to see you, Melanie. Why haven't you called or come over?"

"I've been very busy."

"That's not the only reason, *is* it."

"No. I was sort of in shock over your hypnotherapy session. I don't know what to think about it."

"You don't have to think or figure out anything. I'm not dwelling on it, I'm going on with my life in the present, and enjoying it. I urge you to do the same." I looked into her eyes. They seemed to soften.

"Please give me a kiss for luck before I go back on." She acquiesced and we kissed. Her kiss was as warm as ever. It was then that my hope for our relationship was rekindled.

She smoothed my hair and straightened my bow tie. "After it's over, you must come out to the lobby and let your fans meet you." I didn't have time to speculate about my prospects with her—it was time to go on again. I wowed them, to use a modern term, again and again with my improvisations, astounding even myself.

After my encore and the standing ovation, I left the stage. Melanie met me backstage and we went out to the lobby. People crowded me so much that a couple of ushers cordoned me off and set up a line for them to greet me.

The questions: "How do you improvise so well?" "How can I play like you?"

My only answer was, "Practice, practice, practice for twenty years!"

I tired of the questions quickly and retired to my dressing room. Melanie followed. "You were a hit! We've got it all on video and I'll get a copy for you."

"Thank you, my love," I said as I moved to hold her in my arms.

"Your performance was great, but it would be perfect if you added more genres of music, like jazz and blues."

"What are they?"

She pulled away from me. "You don't know?"

I shook my head. "Sorry, no. I've lived a sheltered life."

"I see I'm going to have to introduce you to You-Tube."

"Who's that?"

"Not who. What."

"Well, introduce me then. You know I want to hear new music."

"I'll come over tomorrow evening. I'll fix dinner for us, then we'll get to work."

I smiled. It was the opening I was hoping for to continue with her. "Can you give me a ride home?"

She hesitated a moment. "All right. We have to get Nick. He's waiting for me in the lobby."

"Why are you still seeing him?"

"I don't think it's any of your business."

10

I was finishing up a draft of the "Melanie" movement of my symphony when I heard a knock at the door. I glanced up at the clock. I was still in my bathrobe.

"Melanie! Can you wait a minute?"

"No! I've got my hands full of groceries! Open the door!"

I tied up my robe and opened the door.

"Still in your bathrobe?"

"I was working on my symphony and lost all track of time."

I took the grocery bags from her and we headed for the kitchen. "Oh my God! This is a mess, Van! You throw all the trash on the floor?"

I set the bags down on the table. "I don't know what to do with it. I've never had to keep house before. Not only that, I was engrossed in composing. What should I do with the trash?"

"You've got two cans here," she indicated with her hands. "This one with the lid is for garbage and this open one is for recyclables."

"What are recyclables?"

"Paper, boxes, cans, bottles. First you have to rinse the cans and bottles."

"Okay, I'll do it now if it pleases you. I really need a housekeeper and cook. Could you find me someone who can cook German food?"

"It would take time to find the right person. I'd have to charge you for my time, but I'll do it."

That would be wonderful!"

She helped me put things in order, loaded the dishwasher, then suggested I get dressed while she prepared the meal.

I returned to the kitchen after I washed and dressed.

"What can I do to help?"

"You can find us a bottle of white wine and a couple of wine glasses."

I set the wine and glasses on the counter. I waited for her to open the bottle because I didn't know how it was done in this century. She looked at me. I looked back, not wanting to reveal my lack of knowledge about opening the wine. After a moment she fished out an opener from a drawer and opened the wine while I watched. *I must be able to do that next time. I can't appear to be so ignorant. Every man must know how to open a bottle of wine.*

We sipped some wine and she added some to the chicken dish she was cooking on the stove. "You could get me some lettuce, tomato, and carrot out of the fridge. We'll have a salad."

"At your service, mademoiselle." I bowed with a courtly flourish. She smiled. *Good. I am making an inroad, helping her feel comfortable with me again.*

We dined at the kitchen table. "This is delicious," I said of the chicken. "You are a marvelous cook. I wish you'd cook for me more often."

"I'm not a professional cook, and I've got school to finish. It takes up most of my time."

"I know. I was just daydreaming. Any time you have for me makes me very happy."

Again she smiled. *I will keep working on pleasing her and maybe she'll stop seeing that milksop, what's his name . . . Nick.*

After I helped her clear the table and fill the dishwasher, we retired to the music room with a fine old port that I had found in the wine closet.

She played a lovely Debussy *Ballade* and I played some lighthearted melody I made up on the spot.

"That's beautiful," she said. "I've never heard it before. Who wrote it?"

I joined her on the couch. "I just now made that up for you. You're an inspiration to me. You even inspired one of the movements of my symphony." Well, we didn't get around to YouTube. We wound up in the bedroom instead, thank Heaven!

༺

Melanie did not rush off the next morning, but stayed to show me YouTube. We went in the "office," as she called it. She sat down at the desk in front of a thing with a black front and told me to pull up a chair. She pressed something on the back of the thing and it lit up! I suppose you know how these computers work, so I won't go into detail. I was astounded at this instrument of knowledge. The first thing she did was set up an account for me. Then she showed me how to search for music on YouTube. I wrote down the steps for future exploration.

She uploaded a copy of my concert so I could watch it later, and perhaps others would watch it as well. Then we listened to jazz and blues—very unusual. A far cry from the music of my day, yet it was interesting. Lively at times, other times it was mournful or sensual. Perhaps adding some of those flavors to my music would help modernize my style.

11

I heard a strident knock at the door. Hoping it would be Melanie, I rushed to the door and eagerly flung it open. A stout woman of about sixty years of age, with graying hair and glasses stood before me.

"I'm Bertha, your new housekeeper." *She has a German accent! Maybe I will finally have some German food.*

"Come in! I'm so happy to see you, Bertha!"

She looked me up and down. "You are not dressed yet? Still in a bathrobe at this hour? I hope this does not mean you are a lazy person."

"Oh no." Already I was feeling I must appease her or she would leave. "I often compose in my robe. It is more comfortable and allows me to think more freely."

"Hmph," she replied, skeptical of my protest.

I led her to the kitchen. "You could start in here, I think."

She surveyed the mess. A little imperiously she said, "I will look around the house and decide how much I will charge you. Then I will decide where to start. You can go on with your composing. In future I trust you will be fully dressed when I arrive."

The moment I sat down at the piano I heard her screaming, *"Mein Gott! O Mein Gott!"*

I didn't know what to think. Was she hurt? Did she find an infestation of rats? I ran to find her. She was in the bathroom, shaking her head and muttering, *"Mein Gott, Mein Gott.* A filthy pig."

"A pig?" *How could a pig get in my bathroom?* "Where?"

She shook her finger at me. "There! You are the pig, Herr Bevin. Look at this!" She pointed at the overflowing toilet.

I shrugged my shoulders. "It got clogged, I didn't know what to do about it. I've never had to fend for myself in household matters before."

"You don't keep using it when it's clogged! I will show you how to fix it this time, but if I ever find it this way again, I will quit!"

"I promise, Bertha. I will never do it again."

She shook her finger at me. "You'd better not."

She showed me how to use the plunger to unclog the toilet.

"By the way, Bertha, can you get me a chamber pot for the piano room? I don't want to go back and forth to the bathroom when I'm composing."

Bertha's mouth fell open and she stared wide-eyed at me. She shook her head. "NO! No one but no one uses chamber pots. I will not empty one, nor will I even work for someone who uses one. It is unsanitary and disgusting, to say the least! Only the laziest person in the world would make such a suggestion!" With that said, she left the room.

Bertha has a habit of feeding the birds. She has hung a bird feeder on the patio. She also scatters seed on the ground. "I've never seen anyone put out seed for wild birds. Why do you do that?"

"Lots of people feed birds. They bring joy to our lives. There's not enough wild land for them to live off of around here. We have to help them out. A little squirrel comes around and I feed him, too."

"Do you cook squirrel?"

Bertha laughed. "No. Sometimes my aunt and uncle cooked squirrel for me when I was a child. It tasted like chicken."

"What about the birds? Do you cook them?"

"No, Mr. Bevin. I wouldn't think of it. I just enjoy watching them and listening to them."

"Oh," I said. I didn't want to appear a mean-spirited, selfish man, so I let her continue with the daily routine. Strangely, Bertha's feeding of the wildlife eventually led to a dreadful incident that inspired me later to write a piece dedicated to the little squirrel.

Bertha wanted two days off a week. This luxury was unheard of in the old days, but she said most people get two days off a week. She only worked for me a few hours a day as it was, and now she wanted two days off! She also wanted me to feed the birds on her two days off. What could I say? I was in desperate need of her, so

I agreed to let her have the two days off and to feed the birds. The weather was mild and sunny, so it wasn't a bad thing. It made me take a break from my composing. Otherwise, I would have just kept on and on until my hand cramped up and I was utterly exhausted.

The birds were always eager for the birdseed. The moment I scattered it on the patio, they swooped in from the trees—little gray and brown birds with black heads, larger brown birds with bright orange chests. They would fly away when big blue birds with black topknots showed up. Another little visitor would soon arrive. It was a tiny gray squirrel, barely old enough to be away from its mother. As small as it was, it was fearless in chasing away the birds, even the big blue ones. The squirrel would eat a few large seeds, then it would take one seed at a time and scamper off with it to bury it in the dirt and the fallen leaves. It performed this task most of the day.

I must confess I became attached to the little fellow. I delighted in its antics of scampering around and charging up and down the trees. I began to linger on the patio longer and longer, throwing out extra seed for the birds and the squirrel.

Melanie suggested I take driving lessons so I wouldn't have pay for a driver or cabs. My money wouldn't last forever, she told me; I should begin to economize. There was no guarantee I would ever make enough money from music to live on. The music world today was a very competitive one.

Unfortunately, I took her advice. The driving instructor took me to an empty parking lot for my first lesson. Cars seemed too complicated; I didn't know if I would ever be able to drive one. I scared the wits out of the instructor as well as myself a few times, but eventually I got the hang of it. After several lessons, I felt ready to take Melanie for a drive along quiet country roads.

"There's a winery not far from here with picnic grounds," she suggested. "I could bring a picnic lunch." This sounded pleasant and romantic, so I agreed. She came by my house while I was feeding the squirrel and the birds.

"How sweet! You feed the birds."

"Bertha started this. She asked me to feed them while she's away. See the little squirrel? He's a lively little fellow."

"He's cute all right." She smiled and rubbed my arm gently. I was glad my feeding of the wildlife pleased her.

I put the bag of birdseed in the kitchen and we went out to the garage. Feeling proud of myself for my driving accomplishment, I got into the driver's seat, opened the garage door, and started up the engine. "Here we go," I said as I pushed a little too hard on the accelerator. I pulled out of the garage and started down the driveway. At that very moment the little squirrel dashed right under my wheel. By the time I could hit the brakes, he was flattened. I jumped out of the car, and so did Melanie.

"My God! What have I done? Poor little fellow. Why did he have to run in front of the car?"

"They do it all the time. They're just too fast. It's so terrible."

I no longer wanted to go on a picnic. Melanie wrapped the little squirrel in a towel from the kitchen and I got a shovel from the garage. We buried him under a tree. Although I still felt obliged to feed the birds, I no longer enjoyed it. In fact, it was painful to have to go out there at all. I just filled the bird feeder and scattered the seed as quickly as possible, then went back inside. It may sound silly that I mourned over a squirrel, but there it is. He had been my little friend.

After a couple of weeks my sadness lifted and I fondly remembered his playful scampering about. I felt moved to write an ensemble piece called "Dance of the Squirrels."

~

Bertha had yet another request, or should I say a demand. She wanted to take four days off in a row to visit her daughter and family for the Thanksgiving holiday. I hadn't known a special day had been set aside to give thanks in this country. I gave thanks every day before my meals.

Four days on my own! I didn't want to eat frozen dinners four days in a row, so I called Melanie. Food wasn't the only reason I called her. It was a good excuse to see her. "Will you come over for Thanksgiving? I've missed you so much."

"I can't. I've been invited to have Thanksgiving dinner with Nick's family. My parents are too far away. As it is, it's a day's drive to his family. I'll be gone a few days." *Nick? Nick's family?*

"Why them? Why not me? We could have a cozy little dinner, just the two of us."

"It's a family holiday. I want to celebrate in a family gathering."

A family celebration. I felt left out, alone. Everyone was going to celebrate together and I was going to be alone. Well, I wouldn't eat frozen dinner at home. I would go out to a tavern or inn somewhere. I searched the Internet for a likely place. Yes, Melanie had taught me how to search for things besides music. Thursday noon I called for a cab. I have not wanted to drive my car since I killed the poor little squirrel.

Dining at the hotel was almost worse than staying home. Everyone was dining with family or friends. I was the only one alone. It reminded me that I had been cut off from my friends when I died. Why did I bother coming back? My Immortal Beloved was dining with another man and his family. I have no friends except for Melanie, who might yet abandon me completely. I could think of only one reason to be thankful—the food. Turkey, dressing, potatoes and green beans. A good German wine. A delicious American treat of pumpkin pie. The coffee, however, was weak.

12

"Is it true you have a briefcase with a sign that says it has a quantum field and particles inside?" It was Nick the physicist questioning me. Melanie had invited me to a cocktail party given by one of her professors. Most of the guests were professors or graduate students of various disciplines and their spouses. Unfortunately, Nick was one of the guests. Melanie had disappeared into a group of chatty colleagues, leaving me alone with the irritating Nick.

"Did Melanie tell you that?" Nick nodded. "Did she tell you I also have a football which hit me on the head and caused me to lose my memory?"

"Melanie tells me everything."

I wonder. Did she tell you we have slept together and she is madly in love with me? "I have the case, but I remember nothing about it. Doubtless a practical joke."

"I would have to agree with that. There is no known way of encasing a quantum field in a briefcase. Probably some silly prank of an undergraduate. I'd like to see it though. It might be good for a laugh."

"Excuse me, Nick, but I must get some food." I needed to get away from my rival. I had no desire to converse with him. I felt more like punching him in the nose than talking. He followed me to the buffet table.

"How about Melanie and I come over tomorrow and take a look at it?"

"It's locked—with combination locks. You won't be able to see much."

"I want to see it anyway."

I filled a little plate with hors d'oeuvres. I didn't think I could stop him from eventually seeing it, so I acquiesced. I thought he would leave me alone after I agreed. I started eating the delectable small bites as I walked away from him. That didn't stop him.

"What you do know about quantum fields, Van?"

"I know nothing. I'm a composer. I only know fields of music."

"Quantum particles are . . . " He droned on. I wasn't listening. I saw Melanie emerge from her group and I hastened to her side. Nick was right behind me.

"Melanie. When do you think we can leave? I need to get home soon."

"Not yet, Van. I want you to meet some of the people in the Music Department."

"Very well," I agreed reluctantly. I knew next to nothing of today's music and feared making a fool of myself in conversation with them. I planned to control the conversations by asking them questions before they could ask me. Melanie introduced me to the Chair of the Music Department, Ellen Berkowitz, a woman! Women are everywhere these days it seems.

"I heard you play at Thompson Hall. You were truly marvelous. Where did you study?"

Already I had lost control. She was asking questions. "In Vienna."

"Which school?"

In my earlier life there was no university such as this one in which to study music. I studied directly with composers and with my own ears as long as I could hear. I clumsily changed the subject. "I must ask you, is it difficult to be in charge of the Music Department?"

"Well, not usually. Occasionally, though, situations arise which require complicated solutions."

"Do you find it difficult to have to listen to students' compositions? Doesn't it assault your ears and your musical soul?"

Ellen laughed. "Sometimes it does, but an occasional prodigy makes it worthwhile. Actually, it's always worthwhile to be involved in the growth and advancement of any student who makes an effort."

"Ah," I said. I hesitated just long enough for Ellen to get a question in.

"What genres of music does your expertise lie in, Van?"

"Well, um, I'm most knowledgeable about classical music."

"Oh, Mozart, Bach, Beethoven, Brahms . . . "

"Brahms? He must have been after my time." *I said the wrong thing! I have to get off the one subject I thought I knew all about.*

"Brahms was *after* your time? What do you mean?"

"Nothing. I've started to study jazz and blues. More of a beginner in those areas."

"I'd like to hear you play some jazz."

I winced at the question. I had to get away from her questions.

"What's the matter?"

"I'm getting a headache. I'd better go home and lie down." I turned abruptly and went in search of Melanie.

"I have a headache," I told Melanie when I found her. "I must go home."

"You do? I thought your head didn't hurt any more."

"It's started up again. Please, take me home."

She agreed, but the ubiquitous Nick came along with us. "Why not let me look at the briefcase now, Van? Then we won't have to come over tomorrow."

"I'm not up to it right now. Tomorrow will be soon enough."

～

I heard his loud, impatient knock at the door. It was eight-thirty in the morning! I did not expect them so early. I was still in my bathrobe. Nick was interrupting my communion with a strong cup of coffee.

I opened the door and glared at Nick. Melanie was behind him. She stepped forward. "Good morning, Van. Sorry we're so early. Nick couldn't wait another minute to see your briefcase."

"It's not that early," Nick protested, looking at his watch. "I've been up since five."

I made way for them to enter. "Do you want some coffee? A pastry?"

"Sounds good to me," Melanie said. We headed for the kitchen.

Nick said, "Where's the briefcase?"

"In the entry closet. I don't want to get it until after our coffee." My protest didn't stop Nick. By the time I got to the kitchen, he had gotten the valise out of the closet. He set it on the kitchen table while I poured the coffee and put some pastries on the table next to the valise.

Nick was examining the locks. "Maybe they used a binary code." He started twirling the number dials.

"Stop! Don't open it!!"

"Why not, if there's nothing in there?"

"There's nothing in there to interest you. Just all the music notes I will ever write in this lifetime. Only I can let them out!" I grabbed the case.

Nick said, "I heard crackling and popping sounds coming from it when I picked it up. I'm not sure it's safe for you to keep it in the house."

"All the more reason to keep it closed." I returned the case to the closet. I heard a crackling sound as I closed the door.

"You should let me take it to the lab and inspect it for safety reasons."

"NO!"

Since Nick couldn't open the case, he quickly downed his coffee and a pastry, then rushed Melanie out the door with a muffled "See ya."

13

*C*hristmas alone. Melanie has gone to visit her family. Bertha has gone to her family. I have never felt so alone as I do this Christmas. I have no one except Melanie—and she has abandoned me on Christmas.

Although I do not long for my old life, at least there I had a social life when young. As a young pianist and teacher, I taught the wealthy. They attended my concerts and invited me to their soirées. It was exciting. As I grew harder and harder of hearing, though, I eschewed the social life and the teaching. They would laugh to think of a deaf musician. Still, I had some friends.

Some things have not changed the way I would have wished. Everything here is always strange, even Melanie. I profess to love her, often I feel it. Other times, I feel two hundred years away from her and her world. Even with her friendship, I am alone. She doesn't know I am from another century. I have to pretend with her. I can't be myself. Being here is harder than I had imagined in Elysium. I am now only really happy playing the piano or composing, much like during my past life.

After Christmas, the New Year celebration. Melanie was back and invited me to another party. Of course Nick was there. The lights were bright. The partygoers were drinking glass after glass of champagne, talking and laughing loudly. The music was loud. I drank some champagne, but I didn't feel like laughing. Melanie was dancing with Nick. I could barely tolerate that. I needed some fresh air, quiet, and an uninterrupted view of the stars. Also, I wanted to avoid talking to people and saying something stupid. I stepped out onto the veranda. A biting chill was in the air. The light of the stars was nearly obliterated by the electric lights glittering everywhere. My thoughts and feelings did not improve on the veranda.

14

The new me is completely unknown in the twenty-first century. How can an unknown get a symphony played? It's all very well to play a concert for the local university, and perhaps I could even get the school orchestra to play one movement, but my completed symphony would be beyond them in length and complexity. I have to make a name for myself if I want important orchestras to play it.

The audience had loved my first concert, but it was limited in variety. How to expand my repertoire seems to be my next challenge. I couldn't resist the temptation to listen to improvisations on my own music, so I searched YouTube for those first. There were a few pleasant improvisations and a few not so pleasant.

Then I found one improviser who impressed me very much. I almost thought I was listening to myself. I wondered if he had somehow tapped into my soul. I found his jazz and blues piano compositions also remarkable.

I went on to listen to more blues and jazz pianists, Leonard Bernstein's music, and many more composers. I tried to incorporate their use of chords and rhythms in my improvisations.

After a while I felt I was ready for another concert. Melanie was able to book me at the university again. It was a success. A student made a video of my concert for booking agents.

She uploaded the video to YouTube and contacted a few agents for me and sent them the video link. They were not interested, however. Some wanted virtuosos who played Bach, Beethoven, Chopin, and so on according to the written music. For other agents my music was too "highbrow" for their audiences. I was stuck in no-man's land. I would have to finance my own concerts at first.

Melanie, that dear sweet love of my life, helped me hire a publicist and rent a small auditorium in San Francisco. Even with all the publicity, only eighty people showed up. Fortunately, due to the publicist's efforts there were a few reviewers in the audience. One said my music had a distinct flavor of Beethoven with a twenty-first century style. I got all but one rave review from them.

One reviewer did not think much of improvisers. That attitude is preposterous. In my day a good improviser was highly respected and sought after. The reviewer suggested I improvised because I could not read music or perhaps I was jealous of Beethoven's fame and sought to demean his music.

It was obvious to me that he did not understand music at all or he would have seen I only made my written music better in improvising. One reviewer said as much, saying, "Finally, a composer has gone beyond Beethoven to new heights." Ha! Exactly. Beyond Beethoven! I've gone beyond myself! In my previous life I had said of some of my music that I was writing for audiences of the future. Little did I know then that I would be writing *in* the future.

The good reviews outweighed the one bad one, thus I was able to get a booking at a better venue in San Francisco. About two weeks before the concert, Melanie and I were in the supermarket. There was a line of shoppers ahead of us, so we had to wait a few minutes. Melanie perused the magazines and tabloids to pass the time. I was busy thinking of what I would play at my concert.

"Look at this!" Melanie shoved a tabloid in front of my face. It had a large photo of me on the cover with the caption, "BEETHOVEN'S BACK!"

I took it in my hands. "What is *this*? Who did this? Did Lorraine do this?"

"Shhh. It must have been the interpreter. Lorraine would never do such a thing."

The writer said I claimed to be Beethoven back from the dead and detailed the hypnosis session. Although it was true I was back from the dead, no one was supposed to know. The writer also strongly insinuated that I was insane, with delusions of grandeur.

"I'll be the laughingstock of San Francisco. Now no one will come to my concert. They'll think I'm a charlatan, making up this story to get publicity."

Melanie shrugged her shoulders and motioned me forward as the checker began to scan our items.

◠

The tabloid article has gone viral on the web. Hundreds of people feel free to make stupid comments about me, whom they had never met. They believed what the article said. The publicist tried to counteract them with her own comments, as have Melanie and I. People just made fun of our defenses. I no longer want to give the concert, but Melanie has dissuaded me from canceling.

With only a week to go before the concert, a reporter from a local paper showed up on my doorstep. I was still in my bathrobe and opened the door to get my newspaper. There he was, leaning against the porch railing and squashing my beautiful roses. I hoped the thorns pricked him, but if they did, he didn't seem to notice.

"What do you want?"

He stepped up to me and pulled out a press card. "What about this claim that you're Beethoven?"

"It's not true!" I was fuming! I slammed the door in his face.

He was still talking on the other side of the door. "Did you plant this story to garner interest in your upcoming concert?"

"NO!"

"If you want to refute it, I can print your response in my newspaper."

I opened the door a little. "All right," I said, "but I have to get my coffee. Want some?"

"Sure."

I closed the door and got two cups of coffee. I didn't want a stranger in my home, so I took the coffee outside and joined him on the porch. I explained the football incident and how I had lost my memory. The hypnosis session was intended to help me retrieve my memory.

"How do you explain the fact that you could remember nothing but Beethoven's life?"

"I don't know. The mind plays tricks when we're hypnotized?"

"You're German. Why are you in America?"

"I want to study your music and write my tenth symphony."

"How did the tabloid get hold of your story?"

"I don't know for sure, but I think it was the German student who acted as interpreter of the hypnosis session."

"Why would he do that?"

"Maybe for money? Out of jealousy for my talent? He's a piano student."

"What are your plans while you're here in the U.S.?"

"As I said before, to write my tenth symphony."

"You have written nine symphonies already? You seem awfully young to have accomplished so much."

I smiled and lied. "I got an early start. God has given me a great talent which I must use to the best of my ability for the betterment of mankind."

We talked a little more about how the story had gone viral, about my music and my upcoming concert.

A couple of days later I read his article in the paper. It was good. I hoped it would help to dispel people's doubts about me.

15

So there I was in San Francisco, waiting in my dressing room. Melanie had driven me there. It was the most terrifying ride of my life. Huge trucks and fast cars crowded about us on a multilane freeway while we were going seventy-five miles an hour. In my earlier life it would have taken an entire day and part of the night to go that far in a horse-drawn carriage. Thank God it only took a little over an hour now. Any longer and I might have died from fright.

"Van! Open your eyes a minute and look at the view!" I opened them. San Francisco appeared to rise out of a misty sea like a magical kingdom. Soon we arrived at the Golden Gate Bridge which led to the city. It was unlike anything I had ever seen. Crowded with vehicles of all types, we drove across it. On the left I could see sailboats, some land in the distance. On the right, endless sea. I was petrified that the bridge might collapse and we would be drowned, but I couldn't close my eyes. I was compelled to keep staring in wonder.

Finally, we got across safely to the other side. San Francisco was gargantuan compared to the cities I had known in my previous life. I was astonished at the height of the buildings. I wondered how they could stay upright and not crash to the ground.

Finally we arrived at the concert hall. I went straight to my dressing room to unwind after the stressful trip. I didn't want to see the piano beforehand. Its quality, or should I say possible lack of quality, might cause me more distress. Melanie got me a cup of coffee and then left me alone to relax before the concert.

After introducing me she would be sitting out front. I was worried that no one would come to the concert because of the review which made me sound like a charlatan. Well, maybe I was a charlatan doing silly improvisatory tricks at the piano rather than playing according to the written scores of famous music. I had no idea what the audience, if there was any, would think of me. Would they come because I was a great composer or would they come to laugh at an insane man who thought he was Beethoven?

It was time. I walked out onto the stage, squinting my eyes to get a look through the glaring lights at the audience. There were hundreds of people sitting in row after row in the orchestra section and more in the balcony! I did my usual visual scan of the ebony grand piano as I walked around it. Was it in tune? Could I draw forth the sounds I wanted from it? I sat down at it, stared at the glistening keys. The name-board above the keys said Steinway. Were Stein's descendants still making pianos? I preferred his pianos in my previous life. I hoped it was made by a master and would allow me to coax the best sounds possible from it.

As I played my first piece, I smiled and nodded my head at the resonance of this wonderful piano.

Someone in the front row stood up and pointed at me. He shouted out, "See? He looks like a madman!"

I stopped playing. "Yes, I am mad! I am mad at the man who is disrupting my concert. Will someone please remove him from the audience!" A couple of ushers hustled down the aisle and coaxed the man to leave. The rest of the concert was without incident except for the vigorous and extensive standing ovation at the end.

There were too many people for me to greet them in the lobby, so I stayed in my dressing room awhile. Melanie came in with a man who wanted to be my personal manager. He shook my hand. "George O'Rourke. Your performance was amazing!"

"Thank you," I said.

"I want to talk to you about being your manager."

"What would that entail?"

"I'd get you bookings, perhaps performing in films, composing for films, handle your publicity, advise you in your career."

"That sounds good," I said.

Melanie said, "We'll check your references and call you in a few days."

Melanie and I went back to my place and celebrated my success with champagne and lovemaking.

⌒

George's references checked out, so we had him come over to the house. He was a young man full of enthusiasm. We talked about my goals and I showed him some of my scores.

"I have a network of agencies who can book you around the country."

"It's a big country. I'll be on the road all the time! I don't like riding in cars very much."

"You hop a plane," George said. "Across the country to New York in about five hours."

"A plane?"

"You fly in an airplane, Van," Melanie explained.

"Fly?" I was shaking my head and muttering, "No . . . no . . . no . . . ."

"George asked, "You're not afraid of flying, are you?"

"I don't know. I've never tried it."

George shook his head with some dismay. "How did you get here then? By boat?"

I lied. "Yes. By boat."

"You'll have to fly. Cars or trains are just too slow."

"If Melanie will go with me, I'll fly."

Melanie was shaking her head. "I can't do that. I have school and my Master's thesis."

George said, "I could fly with you the first time, but I have too much work to do to go with you all the time. You'll get used to it. I'll write up our contract and bring it over in a few days." He shook our hands and left.

"I don't know, Melanie. Flying sounds dangerous."

"Nonsense. It's safer than riding in a car."

"That sounds like it's even more dangerous to get in a car. Maybe I'll just stay home all the time."

She laughed and kissed me.

16

While I waited for the concert bookings, I worked on my symphony. I wanted to include a movement expressing my feelings about war, but it would not be the glorifying of war as I had done in my *Sinfonia eroica*. When I had written that one, it was as a tribute to Napoleon. I had thought he was a victorious leader against tyranny, but when I heard he had set himself up as emperor, I saw that he was a tyrannical conqueror himself. Angry and disappointed, I had scratched off the dedication so hard that I made a hole in the paper. It became simply *Sinfonia eroica*. I came to realize war and conquest were not glorious but ugly. There are times we must fight to defend liberty, and it must be for the betterment of humanity.

The movie I had seen of World War II was fresh in my mind. I searched the Internet to learn the reasons for it. Yet another tyrannical conqueror, Hitler, killing millions, and this was only last century. And World War I. And Mao Zedong—millions of his own people. And Stalin. All tyrannical dictators. I could name more but you probably know of them. It was sickening. I had hoped the world would be rid of these demons after the defeat of Napoleon. I had to put off writing the war movement until I recovered from the extreme malaise this new knowledge left me with.

⌒

Divertissement. That is what I sought. I called Melanie. She had some free time. We decided to go wine tasting. I was hesitant to drive because of the sad death of the little squirrel, but Melanie convinced me I could do it, just take it easy on the gas pedal. I pulled out of the garage and down the driveway very slowly. No accidents occurred.

Spring comes early here, so the hillsides were covered in fresh green grass, except for where the grapevines marched across the land.

"Stop rocking the car!"

"What?"

"You're rocking the car. Pushing the pedal up and down like a piano pedal."

"No, I'm not."

"Yes, you are. Just press it steadily so the car goes at an even speed."

"I'll try."

I managed for a few minutes, then she started complaining again. I pulled over to the side of the road. "You drive."

We got out and switched seats. "I don't know why you can't pay attention to your foot," she said.

"It's automatic, I guess. I've been pushing piano pedals for so long, I just can't seem to stop."

We pulled up to a small building amid the vines. "Open for Tasting." We went in. The bartender, or rather "hospitality associate" as his name tag said, was Kevin. He wanted money first, so I paid for two of us to taste a variety of their wines. He poured just a little white wine into our glasses, easy for me to swallow down at one time.

Melanie instructed me otherwise. "Van! Just sip it, savor it. You're not supposed to gulp it down." Kevin poured us another variety of white wine. I did as Melanie had instructed me.

I lifted my glass in a toast to her. "This is a wonderful idea you had. Just the thing to lift my spirits." We chatted pleasantly while we tasted several wines. I liked the pinot noir best and bought a bottle for later, then we headed off to another winery. We tried their wines, then Melanie insisted we find a place for lunch. She said otherwise she would get too drunk to drive.

We found a lovely little cafe on the side of the road. "Giulia's Wine Bistro," the sign declared. Many vineyards permeated this region, just as in France in my earlier life. The food was delightful, and we drank more wine. I was feeling the effects of all that wine, the beautiful weather, beautiful Melanie. It was the most beautiful day of my life, past and present. But, as often happens to us, our perfect lives, if we have been so lucky to attain them, eventually crack and crumble before our very eyes, until only a shadow of our former bliss remains to taunt us.

The wine had loosened my tongue far too much. I spoke very freely, but not freely enough to reveal my past—I spoke about something much worse!

I said, "You said once you weren't ready to marry. Do you still feel that way?"

"I want to get married, but not until after I get my Master's. When I do marry, I want to have children—two of them. Twins would be perfect so I can have them both at one time. A boy and a girl."

"I love children," I said. She smiled softly, then I said the words that ruined my perfect life. "I'd like to have some, too, only I can't sire children."

She looked alarmed. "You can't?"

"That's what I said."

"Who told you that? A doctor?"

"No. Mozart did."

"What?"

I laughed. The truth was unbelievable. "You are right, it was a doctor."

Her mood changed instantly from sweet softness to . . . I don't know what. Her spirit seemed to withdraw.

"I've had enough wine," she said. "Can we go now?"

"What's the matter, Melanie?"

"I want to have a family, children. You can't. I love you. It breaks my heart to say, but I have to think about marrying Nick after I graduate."

"Nick? What if he can't sire children, either? What if you can't have children?"

"Chances are we both can."

"If you can't, you might as well marry the man you really love—me!"

"I've already been examined by a doctor and told there's no obvious reason why I can't."

"What about Nick? Is there a test for him?"

"There is, but I don't want to ask him to take it."

"Melanie, I want you to marry me, and I won't stop asking until he takes the test and the facts are known. Even then, I might not stop trying to see you."

"Oh, Beethoven. Even if he can't, I won't marry you. I wouldn't marry him either if he couldn't have children. I'll find someone else. Now, please, let's go."

We rode home in silence. She stopped the car in front of my house and told me she wouldn't see me again. No amount of pleading would change her mind. I couldn't believe it! What has happened to my perfect life? What good was it for Mozart to give me that damned valise? It was of no good whatsoever!

17

I thought I couldn't live without her. I had no desire left for this life. It didn't matter that I had a manager and the promise of concerts and fame. My tenth symphony no longer mattered. As far as I was concerned, it was over for me in the twenty-first century. The agony I suffered from the loss of Melanie was unbearable. I wanted to die. I remember Mozart saying I might not be allowed back in Heaven if I killed myself. I cried and drank a few glasses of wine. I tried playing the piano, but wound up banging the keys and slamming the keyboard cover down.

Then I had a brilliant idea, or so I thought at the time. *Maybe I can't directly kill myself, but what would be wrong with just going for a long walk in the pouring rain without a coat? If I got lost in the woods and died from exposure? That wouldn't be quite the same as killing myself.*

I stepped out into the night, the pelting rain quickly drenching me. I was shivering from cold, but I kept on going. After a while I couldn't remember why I was out there. I couldn't think of anything but getting warm and dry. I turned around and tried to walk back home, but it was pitch black out and I couldn't see where I was going.

After a few minutes of staggering blindly, I saw a porch light on and went up to the door. At first I thought it was my own house. I tried to open the door but it was locked. Then I saw it was *not* my house, but at that point I didn't care whose house it was. I knocked on the door again and again, but no one answered. I tried to look through a window. I could see light through the curtains. *They must be there. There's a light on. Maybe they'll hear me at the back door.*

I went around back and found another door. I knocked as loudly as I could until my knuckles hurt, but no one answered. I tried the doorknob. The door was unlocked so I went in and called out. Still no one answered. The entry was through the laundry room. *I'll dry my clothes, get warm and try to find my way back home.* My hands were so cold they wouldn't work right. It took some doing to peel off all my wet clothes. I put them in the dryer and turned it on. (Thank God Bertha had shown me how to work the washer and dryer in case I wanted to use them while she was gone.) I was still wet and shivering from the cold. I stumbled from room to room until I found a bed and crawled in.

The next thing I knew, someone was shaking me. I was in the middle of a wild dream. I yelled out, "I am Ludwig van Beethoven, the greatest composer in the world!" Two sheriff's deputies were standing over me. They pulled me out of bed. I was too groggy to resist.

"Where are your clothes?"

"In the dryer."

They made me get dressed, handcuffed me, read me my rights, and took me outside. The couple who lived in the house were standing on the porch. They watched as the deputies put me in the patrol car.

At the station they fingerprinted me and took mug shots. I saw the pictures later. I looked like a wild man. A dead wild man. My hair was wet and scraggly and I was white as a sheet. They put me in the Sobering Center to "sleep it off." I tried to tell them I wasn't very drunk, just despondent over the loss of my Immortal Beloved.

"Yeah, sure," they said, and in I went.

After a while I fell asleep, only to have wild nightmares of wandering in a desert, alone and bereft of any human contact.

⌒

The next morning they gave me some weak coffee, weak scrambled eggs, and limp toast. After that I was allowed to make a phone call. I only knew one person's number—Melanie's. I called her.

"Melanie, don't hang up! I'm in jail! Please help!"

"Why are you in jail?"

"It's a long story. Nothing too serious, but can you come down here and help me?"

"I guess, but this is the last time I can help you with anything. Nick doesn't want me seeing you for any reason."

That cursed Nick. Spoiling my perfect life. "Thank you, my love."

By the time Melanie arrived, the sheriff's department had spoken again with the owners of the house. They understood my predicament at the time and did not wish to press charges. I was released with the strong recommendation that I see a psychotherapist for my emotional troubles.

In the car, Melanie asked, "What happened to you?"

"It's a long story, but I'll give you the short version. I was so distraught over our breakup that I went for a walk last night in the rain. I got lost. I was wet and cold. I knocked on a door but no one answered. The door was unlocked so I went in and called out. No one was home. I put my clothes in the dryer and got in a bed to keep warm until my clothes dried. I fell asleep. The owners came home and called the sheriff. End of story."

"That was quite long enough! You've got to get over me and move on, Van."

She drove me home. I said goodbye in the car and kissed her. She kissed back as warmly as ever. "Please come in just for a cup of coffee? I want to play a new theme from my symphony for you."

"Well, just for a minute. Then I have to get back to Nick."

Nick, Nick, Nick. It drives me crazy!

We went in. Melanie fixed the coffee while I played some bewitching music on the piano. We didn't bother drinking the coffee but wound up in bed. It was an exquisitely sad goodbye.

18

I am on my own now. Melanie has deserted me. It's apparent to me that the stupid quantum field valise has either been damaged or was never anything but a joke. Otherwise, Melanie would be by my side. Trying to end my life surreptitiously didn't work. I now resolve to create my own future as best I can. This decision has lightened my being a little.

I thought it might be a good idea to get out of the house for a while, do something frivolous. The easiest thing I could think of was to go to the grocery store. Bertha did most of the shopping, but I thought it might be enjoyable to browse and find some things on my own. I took along some earplugs in case the music was too obnoxious.

I had driven to the grocery store parking lot with my driving teacher, so I knew the way. It wasn't complicated. I felt confident enough to drive solo. I was a little excited at the prospect of accomplishing this small challenge. I pulled out of the garage very slowly, remembering the tragedy of the little squirrel. I did not want to injure any more little creatures.

On the streets, cars were honking at me because I was driving so slowly. I pulled over often so they could pass. Eventually I got to the store. I was in luck. There was a spot right in front of the grocery store. *Easy spot to pull into.* Unfortunately, when I applied the brake, somehow my shoe was off center of it and pushed the accelerator as well and I plowed right into the fruit stands in front of the store. Fruit was flying everywhere. Fortunately, no one was hurt. A store manager came running out of the store faster than I could get out of the car.

In a a couple of minutes a police car arrived. Two officers got out and came over to me. *Officer Ryan again!* "I didn't mean to do it! I put on the brake but the car kept going."

"Look, Rick," Ryan said to his partner, also of my acquaintance. "It's our old pal Van Bevin, the quantum briefcase guy." The two of them laughed.

"Have you been drinking? Doing drugs?"

"No, I swear not. My foot got off center of the brake pedal and the accelerator was pressed down at the same time."

"Let me see your driver's license and registration."

I took my license out and showed it to him.

"Where's the registration?"

"I don't know."

Ryan sighed in exasperation. "Could it be in the glove box?"

I looked in the glove box and sure enough it was there. I took it out and gave it to him.

He turned to Rick. "Go check for priors."

To me he asked, "Proof of insurance?"

I looked askance at him.

His voice rose a little. "In the glove box?"

I found it. When I handed it to him, he leaned in close to my face and sniffed. "I don't smell any alcohol but you'll have to take a test to see if you're DUI."

"DUI?"

Ryan shook his head. "Driving under the influence of alcohol or drugs."

"What kind of test?"

"Get out of the car." I got out.

He looked into my eyes for a moment. "First, your eyes. They look normal. Now, stand on one leg until I tell you to stop."

"That's easy." I did it well.

"Now walk on this parking spot line here, heel to toe, like this." He demonstrated the instructions. I was a little wobbly because I was nervous, so he made me do it again. I passed, barely.

He looked down at my shoes. "Those sneakers are a little wide. You have to be careful to push only one pedal at a time." He started writing on a little pad. "I have to give you a citation for careless driving."

"What does that mean?"

"It means you'll have to pay a fine. You can appear in court and try to argue that you weren't careless, but if you lose the case, you'll have to pay a fine anyway. You'll get something in the mail that tells you what to do."

Rick came back with a big smile on his face.

"You got something?"

"Yeah. He was picked up for unlawful entry, sleeping in the owners' bed, and using their clothes dryer.

Claimed he got lost in a rain storm. The owner didn't want to press charges."

"Well, that doesn't count then. Why's it so funny?"

"When the deputies woke him up, he claimed he was Beethoven, the greatest composer in the world."

"That *is* funny."

"I was having a dream. I didn't really believe it!"

"Okay, Beethoven. Try to stay out of trouble now."

I exchanged insurance information with the manager of the store and apologized profusely. Then he helped me call a tow truck to take my car to the repair shop. I never did get to the grocery store.

⌒

While my car was in the repair shop, I worked on my symphony. The movement I was working on was tinged with sorrow. At first I didn't like it and kept tossing ruined scores on the floor, one after another. Why couldn't I write something happy? Because I wasn't happy without Melanie. Finally, I accepted that this movement would be a melancholy one and went on to write it. Everyone has suffered at one time or another. I figured listeners would connect with it. It was a part of life. By now I had stacks of scores for the symphony and for ensembles all over the piano room, the rejected pages scattered on the floor. I had progressed nicely with my symphony so far.

Needing a break, I took a cab to do the shopping I had started out to do when I had wrecked my car. I left Bertha cleaning the house. It was a distraction for me when she was there. She often got in my way or I in hers, so going out seemed an ideal solution.

I wore earplugs in the store so their ghastly music wouldn't bother me. I bought some French wine, pastries, and espresso beans. Also some blackberry preserves. Then I went home.

Bertha was in the kitchen preparing dinner.

"Bertha," I said, "I got a few groceries. Could you put them away for me, please?"

"Sure, Mr. Bevin. While you were out, I straightened up your piano room a bit and removed the dirty dishes. It was a mess!"

"I told you to leave that room alone!"

"It has to be cleaned once in a while. Otherwise you will get silverfish eating your scores and rats eating your spoiled food."

"Hmph!" I hurried to the piano room to see what she had done. All my scores had been put into one tall stack. All the throw-away pages had been mixed in with them!

I was fuming! "Bertha! What have you done?"

She came running,. "What is it? What's the matter?"

"You mixed up all my scores, that's what! You're fired! Now get out of my house!"

"You're a filthy pig and I don't want to work for you anyway! Good luck finding someone else to clean up your messes! She put on her coat and charged out the door, slamming it behind her. What a fine mess I am in now. First, no Melanie, now no Bertha. I have to find another housekeeper. Another distraction to delay the completion of my symphony.

⌒

I didn't know where to find another housekeeper, so I called Bertha and apologized profusely for my loss of temper. She forgave me and said she would come back. She promised not to touch my scores again even though it distressed her to see a room in such disarray. She would, however, remove any dirty dishes she found there.

Then I called Melanie. She didn't answer. I left her a message. "Melanie, love of my life, I will love you eternally. If you change your mind about me, please call, day or night, two years from now or twenty. I love you . . . in case you wonder who this is, it's Beethoven calling." She did not return my call.

I needed a break from wrestling with the scores Bertha had mixed up. I thought I would amuse myself by listening to some recordings of my own works on YouTube.

The first thing that came up was a video of my entry into the twenty-first century! It was titled *Is this Beethoven?* The video clip started just before I appeared on the football field. The field was empty at that spot, then I faded in. There I was, walking along, the valise attached to my wrist. Hit by the ball, down on the ground, up again and running in the opposite direction. The announcer was saying, "Who's that man? He just appeared out of nowhere on the field!" I don't know who posted the video. Was it the German interpreter? Someone who had read the tabloid?

Perhaps I could use this video as proof that I was indeed Beethoven returning to Earth. I won't rush into anything, though. I will think about it. People still might not believe me. Maybe I could ask George his opinion. Then again, he might think I'm crazy and abandon me.

I decided to call Melanie and tell her about it. She didn't answer, so I hung up. I've gotten so used to hiding my true identity, I'm not sure I want to reveal the real me. I think I should wait awhile to tell anyone.

19

It was time to board the plane. I had a concert to give in Los Angeles. I was already a nervous wreck from riding in my car all the way to the airport. George was driving, taking the curves at an insane speed. He had suggested we fly out of the Sonoma County airport since it was closer and the airport less hectic than San Francisco. I said whatever helps me be less nervous on my first plane ride.

The noise of the plane engines was so loud as we walked outside across the tarmac—I had to plug my ears with my fingers. We were greeted cordially by the flight attendant, a vivacious blonde woman. I preferred seats up front but George said the only seats available were near the rear of the plane. To assuage my irritation, he said it was somewhat safer in case of a crash.

A crash! I didn't think anywhere would be safe if we fell out of the sky. Life would be over in a few seconds, and I hadn't finished my symphony! I was scared before, but now I was petrified. The vision of a flaming end was before my eyes. I was shaking as I sat down.

"George. Let's get off the plane and drive down to L.A. It would be much safer."

"No, it wouldn't. More people die in car accidents than in airplanes. Don't worry. Not much can go wrong. The last accident on a plane like this was a few years ago when part of the roof flew off."

"OH MY GOD!" I tried to get up but George pulled me back down.

George said, "I was just kidding." (Later I learned he wasn't kidding. It had really happened.)

I had an aisle seat. I strapped my seatbelt in place and stared out the window beyond George. Pretty soon the flight attendant was giving instructions about what to do in case we crashed.

"Why is she doing that if it's so safe?"

"It's regulations. It's only a slim possibility we'll need to know this stuff. Don't worry, Van. Get a glass of wine when they serve drinks and you'll be all right."

"I'll need four or five glasses to be all right."

The noise of the engines increased and the plane started moving. I wanted to get off the plane. I could see out the window that we were going faster and faster. Then I felt the plane tilt up. I had to get off! I unbuckled my seatbelt and lurched toward the back door. George and the attendants were out of their seats in an instant and tackling me as I reached the door.

"Sir! You have to get back in your seat now!"

I was wrestling with them and screaming. "Let me out! I gotta get out of here!"

"Okay! Okay! We'll get you off the plane, but we're in the air now. You have to wait until we land. Just a few more minutes. Sit down! We're going to land."

We landed and I was escorted off the plane. George got off, too. I ran ahead of him to the car and got in the driver's seat. George had the key so I just sat there trying to regain my composure. George opened my door.

"Get out, Van. I'm driving." I obeyed, and we left for L.A. Although I was quiet, George knew I was nervous riding in the car. We stopped at a bar and he got me a couple of whiskies. Powerful drinks! I was calm for a couple of hours, then we stopped again for lunch and a couple more drinks for me.

"You're going to have to get over your fear of flying, Van. Some of your gigs would take several days to get to by car. I think I have a solution. "

"Tell me."

"You go to a doctor and get a prescription for a tranquilizer."

"What's that?"

"A little pill you take before the flight." It's far more relaxing than alcohol, and you won't be drunk, just a little blissful. Nothing will rattle you."

"Like laudanum?"

"George laughed. "No, not like laudanum. What century are *you* from?"

"The nineteenth. I'll think about it."

"Think hard, because I can't drive you to every gig. If you don't tour, you'll never get well known enough to get your symphony performed. I have to warn you that you can't drink alcohol when you take tranquilizers. It could be fatal."

I decided it was worth a try, and made the doctor's appointment after I got back from L.A.

George was right. The tranquilizers worked perfectly. On my next flight, to San Diego, I was so calm that I fell asleep and didn't wake up until we landed.

I was well received at my concerts. I got great reviews, but there was always the one reviewer who thought me a charlatan. Even the one bad review seemed to draw people who wanted to see me to prove him right. They discovered I wasn't a charlatan at all, but the most amazing improviser ever.

⁊

The video of me on the football field went viral on the web. People were debating in the comments whether it was genuine or if it had been edited to place me in the field. Plenty of people who were there that day responded saying they saw it with their own eyes. I started getting calls from TV talk show producers wanting to interview me on TV. I referred them to George.

"This is pretty good stuff, Van. Free publicity. You should go on these talk shows. Aside from talking, they'll want you to play the piano. Millions of people will see you and hear some of your music."

"I don't know. What would I say?"

"Tell the truth. What is the truth?"

"I thought I knew the truth, but I'm beginning to wonder. Maybe it's all a dream."

"It doesn't matter. Pick whatever truth you want for yourself, but let *them* wonder. It's the mystery that's important. This is great free publicity!"

"Maybe you're right, George."

"I know I'm right. I've already gotten calls to book you in New York. I'll get you booked on a talk show or two while you're there. It will be a few months until your concert, though. I'll go to New York with you."

George is the closest thing to a friend I have now that Melanie has abandoned me. Maybe soon I will have more.

20

My broken heart is mending. Life is beginning to be pleasant again. Flowers are blooming. The birds are singing.

I have been whiling away the time writing love songs in a more modern manner, most of which are too sappy to publish. A few good ones though. They're all about Melanie. I also have been writing her letters, hoping she would come back to me. I have received no response, but at least they haven't been returned. I imagined her reading them and weeping over our lost love. How I miss her! I left her phone messages from time to time but she didn't call back.

I have recovered enough to desire some new female companionship. I wondered if there were other women at the university who might be interested in spending time with me. Yes, I was also thinking maybe I would see Melanie while I was there.

There were girls, girls, and more girls on the campus. That's what they were, girls—barely adults. Many were very attractive, but I preferred just a little more maturity. I didn't want the silliness that often accompanies the very young. I ambled through the halls of the music building, smiling often at women I passed. Some smiled back. One in particular looked me rather boldly in the eye. I felt I had known her before, maybe in my last life. She was carrying a cello case. I had to think quickly of something to stop her, something to ask her.

"Are you a cellist?"

She stopped and smiled. "Yes."

"I'm a pianist. Do you have time for a little duet?"

"I know who you are—Van Bevin. I attended one of your concerts. I'm Carina. I'd love to play with you. Come with me. We have to get a key to a room."

We went down the hall to a small office. Who was there but Melanie! She was talking to the woman behind the desk. "Melanie!"

She turned and stared at me, then Carina. "Hi, Carina . . . Van."

"We're going to play together," I said.

"How nice for you," she said coldly. She passed us and went out the door. I looked after her a little too long, and Carina noticed. She got the key and we left the office.

"So, you and Melanie . . . "

"What do you mean?"

"She was rather short with you. A lovers' quarrel?"

"No. We just uh . . . well, it's over. A brief relationship, now in the past."

Inside the practice room was a small grand, a piano bench, a chair, some music stands in the corner. While she was taking her cello out of its case, I sat down at the piano and played a little to check it out. It was not great, but it would do.

"Do you have any music with you, Carina? By the way, that is a beautiful name—for a beautiful woman."

She blushed a little, smiled. "I have some here in my binder."

I wanted to play it safe with the music. "Do you have any Beethoven in there?"

"Yes." Here's one."

I propped my copy on the piano. "One of my favorites. You must be very skilled to have mastered it. Are you a teacher or a student?"

"I'm a teacher, but I'm always learning."

I looked over the music quickly. I hadn't seen it or played it in a very long time. I hoped I would be up to it. It was a difficult piece. We played the slow, delicate beginning. She had beautiful intonation, sensitive bowing. Marvelous! As the piece progressed and became more passionate, she was definitely up to the task. I was playing right along, listening to the blending of our instruments, when suddenly I heard something else. I kept shaking my head, trying to stop the foreign sounds impinging on the music being played, but I couldn't stop it. I stopped playing and started rubbing my temples, trying to stop the powerful, ominous theme.

"What's the matter?"

I got up from the piano. "I must go!" I left her staring after me as I rushed out the door and down the hall.

It was the war movement! It had broken suddenly into my mind. I had to write it down before it got away. I could not count on recalling it again. I had a music notebook in my car. I sat there and wrote down what I heard, the instruments, the themes, page after page until I ran out of paper. Then I went home to work on it in detail.

I hadn't even stopped to get her phone number. If she was a teacher, I could find her again. The music, however, could have gotten away in a minute.

I worked steadily on the movement for a few days. I was so engrossed I forgot to eat, bathe, change my clothes or sleep. Eventually I fell asleep at my desk, pen in hand. Bertha found me there.

"Mr. Bevin!" Bertha was shaking my shoulder. "Mr. Bevin!" Wake up!"

I struggled to come to my senses. "What?"

"You fell asleep."

"Oh, yes. Well, I'd better get back to work."

"No! You stink! You are going to shower and change your clothes. Then I will fix you something to eat."

Bertha took good care of me, maybe sometimes too good, but I was glad she had brought me out of my mania. I looked at the last page I had been working on. It was a mess and made no sense. I ripped it up and did as I was told. Obviously I needed a break from composing.

I washed, dressed, and ate lunch, then headed back to the school to find Carina again. I walked by the practice rooms but couldn't hear a cello. I inquired at the office and got the room number where she was teaching a private lesson. I waited by her room. It wasn't long before the door opened and a young man came out with his cello case. The door was open, but Carina didn't come out, so I ventured in. She was gathering up her things.

"Carina."

"Oh . . . hi, Van."

"I was in the building and thought I would see if you were around."

She smiled. "I am. What happened to you last week?"

"Sorry I left so abruptly. I've been working on a symphony. A movement which had been eluding me suddenly started playing in my head, coaxed out by our duet somehow. I felt compelled to run off and make notes before it vanished."

"That's understandable. I do some composing myself. You can't let it get away."

"Maybe I could buy you a cup of coffee. We could talk music."

"The Student Union has good coffee," she said.

"Do they have espresso?"

"I'm sure they do. I usually have a cappuccino."

"What's that?"

"You don't know? Espresso and steamed milk. I add sugar and sprinkle chocolate powder on top."

"I think I'll stay with espresso."

So, we went to the Student Union. We got our coffees. I tasted the espresso. "Ahh, very good. So what have you composed?"

"Cello solos, piano and cello, a few string quartets. Nothing complicated. I'm pretty much a beginner when it comes to composing."

"I'd like to hear some, or even play the cello piano pieces with you."

"If you're writing a symphony, you're more advanced than I am. I might feel embarrassed to even show them to you."

"I well understand the complexities of composing and the progress one makes over time. I'd be honored to try one out with you. Simple music is often the most beautiful. I have a marvelous Bösendorfer piano at home. We could try out your music there."

Carina looked at me with a knowing grin. She was reading my mind. "I prefer to use one of the rooms here at school for now. I am not in the habit of going home with strange men."

"I'm strange all right, but I was only thinking of playing music with you."

"You're a man. You are probably thinking of other possibilities."

I smiled and did not otherwise respond. We arranged to meet two days later in the practice room where we had first played together.

❧

I waited for her at the door of the practice room. *Here she comes.* "Carina. How are you?"

"Fine." She studied my face a moment. "Has anyone ever said you look a lot like Beethoven, only better looking?"

"No."

"Well, you do. Haven't you noticed?"

"I . . . well, I *have* noticed. In fact, I play it up a little. I wear my hair somewhat like he did when he was young. Sometimes I turn up my collar. It's not entirely an accident."

"Your fans probably like it." She unlocked the door and we went in.

"Did you bring one of your compositions?"

"I did." She got out the music and handed me a copy. I looked it over while she set up her cello.

She asked, "Do you want to play through your part first?"

I shook my head. "No. Let's start."

It was a lovely, uncomplicated, melancholy piece.

"You're a very sensitive soul," I said when we had finished. "It's beautiful, Carina." I didn't have to lie to please her. It was the truth.

She blushed a little. "You're an amazing sight reader."

We played awhile longer, then she said she had to go.

"Could I take you out to dinner some evening . . . this Saturday perhaps?"

"I'd like that."

∽

Saturday arrived. Although I anticipated our first date with some eagerness, I did not feel the same excitement as I did with Melanie. I would settle, though, for second best. Carina was an attractive woman and a wonderful cello player with a musician's soul. What more could I want?

"You've come in a limo? Don't you drive?"

"I have a car. I drive. I haven't been here long, though, and I'm not familiar with the streets. I thought a limo would be less complicated." Carina smiled, her eyes softened. I knew she would soon be mine.

The evening went smoothly. She did not mention anything about my reviews or my hypnosis session, or even my entrance into this time on the football field. Perhaps she would never find out about those things and we could have an easygoing relationship in which I would not have to constantly defend my sanity.

In the limo after dinner I asked her if she wanted to come over to my place for a glass of wine or a cup of coffee. She said she wasn't ready for that, so I took her home and walked her to her door.

I said, "Shall we get together for another duet soon?"

"Yes, at the school. Thursday?"

"You know, I have a marvelous Bösendorfer at home. The sound is far superior to the practice room piano."

She laughed lightly. "I know. You mentioned it before, but for now it's the practice room."

We kissed good night. She was holding her emotions back, unlike Melanie who succumbed easily to my charms. This relationship will take time, but at least she doesn't already have a boyfriend—or does she? I forgot to ask, but it doesn't matter. I would have won Melanie from Nick if only I could sire children. I can win Carina, boyfriend or no boyfriend.

21

After a few more practice sessions, lunches, and dinners, Carina agreed to come to my house to practice, which of course led to lovemaking and deepening of our relationship. We got along so well that after a few weeks we decided to live together. She gave up her rented house and came to live with me.

The first annoying thing she did was to bring a truckload of furniture. "I already have furniture, Carina. There's no room for more."

"Well I can't just throw away my beautiful antiques, Van. I can rearrange things to make room for them. Help me move your couch."

"Move it where?"

"Preferably out to the garage. It's simply too dull and masculine looking." Grudgingly, I helped her move it out to the garage.

"The dining table and chairs have to go. I inherited a beautiful set from my aunt."

"I need a practice room. I think the second bedroom will do."

And so it went until half of my furniture was in the garage. Then she went back to her place to get "just a few more things." Those "things" were a small, yappy dog and a cat. The dog did *not* like me. He kept barking at me. When I tried to approach him, he gave a threatening growl. "This dog can't live here! He keeps barking at me!"

"Don't worry, he'll get used to you." She picked him up and brought him over to me. He stopped growling when she picked him up. "This is Sirius. Go ahead and pet him." I cautiously put my hand out and he bit my finger!

"No, Sirius! Bad dog!" She put him down and led me to the bathroom to tend my wound.

"How am I going to play the piano with this bandage on my finger? How could you bring such an unfriendly cur here!" Before she could reply, my phone rang. It was my manager, George.

"A lucky break, Van. The concert hall where I got you booked for next month had a cancellation for this coming Saturday night. They've already sold out—a popular performer—and need to fill the spot. They may have to refund some tickets, but I think you'll still have a pretty full house."

"I can't do it! This damned dog just bit my finger. I've got a bandage on it."

"It can't be that bad. You can't miss this opportunity, Van. I'm booking our flight and hotel. I'll pick you up Friday morning. Do you have the tranquilizers?"

"Yes, but . . . " He hung up. That was that. I had to go. Carina took me to the emergency room to get my finger treated to make sure it wouldn't get infected.

22

George picked me up at six in the morning. My finger was still sore, but it was better. I sat in a window seat. It was a long flight to New York. Well-tranquilized, I ventured to look out the window. We were above the clouds. Some distance away ominous, towering, magnificent storm clouds rose higher than our plane. The pilot was flying around them. Later I saw the earth below, a patchwork of green and brown with ponds or lakes, tiny houses. Unbelievable that man could fly so high, higher than the birds! People in this century can see so many wonders of Earth that their ancestors never could. I wonder how many appreciate it.

After we checked into our hotel, we took a walk. Manhattan was a most incredibly crowded city. The buildings were even taller than those of San Francisco. The streets were endless streams of taxicabs, with a few passenger cars and small trucks mixed in. We had dinner at a bistro with a good jazz combo. We were served small plates of strange but delicious food. The wines were also delicious.

Concert night. We pulled up to the stage entrance in a limo. "You don't want people to see your finger bandaged, Van. Take if off."

"But I don't want to injure it more."

"Take it off!" I took it off.

Twenty people or so were waiting outside for me. They were taking pictures with their cell phones and waving papers at me for my autograph. George was trying to fend them off. "No pictures!" That didn't stop them from taking pictures, which later appeared on the Internet. George said it was good publicity. He also said the crowds would get worse as my fame increased.

We had arrived too late for me to check the piano before the concert. People were already being seated. We waited in the dressing room until it was time.

When I entered the stage, the audience applauded. I walked slowly around the concert grand for a visual check, then sat down at the piano. It was another Steinway. I started to play and immediately noticed a few keys were out of tune. I was exasperated! How could they *not* have the piano in tune? I couldn't play it that way. I got up and addressed the audience.

"This piano needs some tuning. I'll see what I can do. Please excuse me for a moment." I walked off stage to find out what could be done.

"I'm sorry," the stage manager said. "We have no one here who can tune the piano."

"Do you have any tuning instruments?"

"We have a little kit here for emergencies, but I don't know how to use it."

"I will do it." I took the kit from him. "You must ensure in future that the piano is properly tuned before a performance!"

"We *did* have it tuned."

"Then you must find a better tuner!"

I took the kit onto the stage. I took out a suitable tool and showed it to the audience. "Not only will you hear a magnificent concert but you will also watch me make the sound of the piano magnificent before I play." I went over every key; only a few needed tuning. Then I sat down to play. My sore finger throbbed when I began, but after a minute I was so engrossed in the music that I forgot about it, thank God.

George had suggested I try to inject a little humor somehow into my concerts so for my finale I pulled over the voice mike. "I was watching a fellow on YouTube— you all know what that is? That is the place where you can watch an infinite number of cats acting crazy. Am I right?" They laughed and applauded. *So far, so good.*

"Anyway, I was watching a video of a man playing "Great Balls of Fire" in a cafe. He reminded me of those crazy cats, so I want to entertain you a little with an attempt to emulate his performance. Would you like to see it?"

I got a resounding applause, so I began. It required various antics—standing up, kicking a foot out from time to time, mixing in different songs such as Batman, changing the lyrics to "Catman" some Beethoven, and finally lying down on the floor while playing. They went wild with laughter and applause.

I wasn't sure I liked reducing serious music to this craziness, but the audience loved it. I had set a precedent for my future performances. Audiences will henceforth expect a "crazy cat" treat at the end of every concert.

My next booking in New York was a late-night talk show which was recorded in the afternoon. The host started out by praising my recent concert then suddenly turning the tables on me.

"So this video of you arriving on the football field from Heaven has had more views than your music. Was that a publicity stunt?"

"Not at all, John. I really don't know how I got there. I remember nothing before that."

"You have said you lost your memory."

"Yes, everything in my life before the football field."

"How do you know you're Van Bevin, then?"

"It's on my driver's license, which was in my pocket."

"And the quantum field briefcase?"

"I can only guess it was a practical joke by someone— maybe a physics student."

"What about the hypnosis session?"

"Is nothing private in this world any more?"

John laughed. "We're all pretty much open books since the advent of the Internet. It's a great publicity stunt. I congratulate your publicist."

I don't like where this interview is heading. I thought we'd talk about my music. I've got to steer this conversation to my music.

"Like I said, it wasn't a stunt. This Internet drivel is not important. My music is important. I'm working on my tenth symphony."

"Like Beethoven?"

"No! Not like Beethoven! He wrote only nine. I will soon finish my tenth."

"That's great, Van, but what I want to know is how you doctored that video to make it look like you appeared out of nowhere on the football field."

"I didn't doctor it, or have anyone else doctor it."

"So you are Beethoven returned to Earth?"

"I'm not Beethoven."

"You're lying."

"How can I be lying?"

"You think you're Beethoven so when you tell me you aren't, you're lying. You're a very smart man. Think you can fool me." I had to smile. "There," he said. "You're smiling. It gives you away."

"If it pleases you, I'll say yes, I am Beethoven. But you know it's not true, so why do you want me to say it?"

"We already know you're not, but the question is, do you really know you're not?"

"This is enough of the questions, John. It matters little what anyone thinks about whether I'm Beethoven or not Beethoven. Enjoying the music is what's important. Let me play something for the audience."

I had come across Rimsky-Korsakov's "Flight of the Bumblebee" and found it delightful. I thought it would be amusing to interweave it with some of my own themes in an improvisation. That is what I played on TV. The studio audience loved it.

After that, I bowed and left the stage before John could harass me any more with his questions. I canceled the next talk show appearance against George's advice. I played one more concert in New York, then flew home.

23

I returned home to be greeted by Carina and her yappy little dog. He was especially ferocious when I tried to hug and kiss Carina.

"Put that dog somewhere else. I can't enjoy kissing you while he's jumping on my legs and barking at me."

She put him in the bedroom. "He'll settle down soon. You've been gone a long time and he has to get used to you again."

"Again? He was never used to me in the first place. Find him another home!"

Before she could respond, I took my suitcase into the bedroom where the dog started barking at me again. I shooed him out and shut the door. I lay down for a rest after my long journey. I was just dozing off when I heard Carina playing the cello. It was lulling me to sleep at first, but then I noticed she was playing the same passage over and over and making mistakes. It was driving me crazy. I got up and went to her practice room.

"You keep playing a G natural when it's a G sharp!"

"I know I'm making mistakes. It's a difficult piece. That's why I have to practice it."

"Do it somewhere else! I'm trying to rest!"

After my rest I went into the music room and sat down at the piano. I started playing but the sound was very muffled. The strings didn't vibrate. I looked out at them, and there was Carina's cat having a nap on the strings! I picked the cat up and took her to the door. Carina saw me.

"What are you doing with my cat?"

"I'm putting her out! She was sleeping in the piano!"

"If you'd just close the lid, she couldn't get in there."

"I don't want to close the lid!" I put the cat out and went back to the piano.

Later I went out to the patio to enjoy some fresh air and watch the birds feeding in my yard. Suddenly the cat jumped out from behind a rock and caught a sweet little bird. She carried it off to a corner of the yard and proceeded to eat it!

That did it! I couldn't take any more of Carina and her pets. I told her to move out at as soon as possible. Fortunately, her rental house had not yet been rented to someone else so she was able to move back in.

I must say, if it had been Melanie with those pets, I would have endured them because of my deep love for Melanie, but I didn't feel so deeply about Carina. That made it easier to tell her to leave.

24

*A*lone again, or should I say alone at last. Peace restored to my domicile. Back to my quiet life with only Bertha to disturb me. The meals she prepares are well worth the occasional disturbance she causes by reprimanding me for my slothfulness.

After a brief respite at home, I took off again for Bonn and Vienna. I was excited to be returning to the cities of my previous life. As usual, George accompanied me. I will not bore you with the details of our flight or my concert.

I had been concerned that in Bonn and in Vienna the public would feel affronted by my toying with "the Master's" works. However, they appreciated my abilities greatly and saw me as another German musical genius. Had it not been for the humor I injected into my concerts though, I may have been less well accepted by the traditional classical music world. As it was, they happily compared me to another comedic virtuoso, Victor Borge.

~

George was looking at a guide book of Bonn. "You'd like this, Van. There's a Beethoven Monument, a huge bronze statue on the Münsterplatz. In 1845 they were going to have the unveiling at a three-day Beethoven festival, but there was no concert hall large enough to accommodate the crowd that want to attend, so they built Beethoven Hall."

"There's a Beethoven Monument? A Beethoven Hall? Incredibly wonderful! We must see it!"

"You didn't know?"

"I didn't remember. Let's see it!"

"There's also Beethoven-Haus Museum, in the building where Beethoven grew up."

We took a taxi through Bonn to the monument. Many buildings from my earlier life were still standing, but Bonn had grown much larger in almost two hundred years. It was beautiful. The streets were paved now. No more muddy wagon wheel ruts to trip in

When we arrived at the monument, I was awestruck. I could barely hold back the tears. We took a look inside Beethoven Hall, then walked over to the Beethoven-Haus. This was the building I where I had been born and grew up! Inside were so many things of mine—music scores, my viola, the organ I played as a child.

"George, look! My desk!"

He was taken aback, then he tried to smile. "Your desk, Van? You're joking, aren't you?"

I recovered fast. "Oh, yes. A little joke. Ah, there's the travel desk Beethoven used."

George nodded, but he was looking at me. Probably wondering if I'd completely lost my mind. I had to try to stay calm and be Van Bevin, not Beethoven.

"Prince Lichnowsky's instruments that he kindly gave to m . . . m . . . him."

George was shaking his head, thinking something, probably not good. *I would have to try harder.* I saw my collection of ear trumpets. I smiled to myself, kept my mouth shut, but oh how happy I was I didn't need those any more! My deafness was probably the worst trial of my life, sent by God or the Devil, I don't know which. Then there was my piano built by Conrad Graf. I was so excited to see it there, but I dared not say the wrong thing.

The honor bestowed on me overwhelmed me. I could not hold back my tears.

"What's the matter?"

"Such an honor," was all I could manage to say.

"Yes," the people of Bonn have always revered Beethoven as the greatest composer that ever lived."

George's response only brought more tears. I wandered away from him to try to try to gain control of my emotions. I succeeded after a couple of minutes and came back to the Conrad Graf piano.

The keyboard looked so small now that I was used to eighty-eight keys. Still, I wanted to play it. "George, I'm going to see what it sounds like, play it a little."

"It's very old. Just for display. They won't allow it."

"Nonsense!" I started to play it. It sounded very tinny and out of tune. A woman wearing a name badge came hurrying over.

"Sir, you may not play this piano! It is very old and delicate. We can't allow it."

"You don't understand! I must play it!"

The woman shook her head. "I'm so sorry, sir, but no."

"Maybe you'll let me play the Broadwood."

"It's not here," she said.

"Where is it?"

It's in Hungary, in the National Museum."

"Why is it in Hungary and not here?!"

"Keep it down, Van."

"Sir, you must talk quietly here. This is a museum. You are startling people. Carl Spina, the publisher, gave it to Liszt."

"Liszt? That child I met . . . oh, Liszt, of course. Who better to have it. He became a great pianist, then?"

She smiled. Yes."

"Excuse me, Van, but we'd better get going."

"All right. I've seen everything here I wanted to see."

Outside, George said, "You were acting strange in there. Seemed to think you were Beethoven."

"You're talking so low I can't understand you. Speak up, man."

He raised his voice, "You were acting strange in there. Seemed to think you were Beethoven."

"Not so loud. Somebody might hear. A ridiculous idea I was just temporarily immersed in his . . . his . . . life."

෴

There was one disturbing event while I was in Bonn which still irritates me. I find it hard to believe that a woman would go to such lengths to get money by creating a lie about me.

George and I walked out one afternoon to a local cafe for a cup of coffee. As soon as we sat down, a woman and a little boy came up to us and sat down at our table without invitation.

"Hello, Van," she said in German. "It's about time you came back to Bonn. This is your son, Ludwig."

"I don't know you, and I never had a child with you."

"You didn't know about the child because we were only together one night. When I found out I was pregnant, I couldn't find you to tell you."

"I was never with you. I have never seen you before."

"How would you know if you have amnesia?"

I was supposed to have lost my memory, so how can I defend myself against this accusation? "I remember some things. I would not have forgotten being with such a beautiful woman as you."

"Ha! I want some financial support for Ludwig."

"Well, you are not going to get it from me. It's impossible for me to sire children. I am physically unable to do so."

"What a stupid excuse. I'm going to bring a paternity suit against you for child support, and what's more, I'm going to tell the press about it. It will ruin you!"

George doesn't speak German, so he didn't know what was going on, except our argument was getting heated. "Go away and leave him alone, lady!"

The manager came over and told her to stop bothering customers. He ushered her and her child out the door.

She called out to me as she left, "You'll be sorry!"

George asked, "What was that about?"

"She accused me of being that boy's father."

"Are you?"

"NO! I never saw her before!"

"Maybe you just don't remember."

"It doesn't matter. I can't be the father of any child."

She wasted no time telling the press. The next day it was in the papers.

"How can I put an end to this accusation?"

"If she takes you to court, you'd have to get a DNA test to prove her wrong. Maybe you should get one now to speed up the proceedings." I wanted to quickly put this matter to rest before she could take me to court, so I got a DNA test. It turned out not to be necessary because there was never any court action.

~

While in Vienna we did some sightseeing. There were so many of my old haunts still standing and in use. The Theater an der Wien has a memorial to me on the first floor. They still perform my symphonies there. I would have liked to attend one, but our schedule didn't allow time for it.

Then there is Zum Schwarzen-Kameel, the restaurant which used to deliver wine, sugar, and coffee to my home. George and I stopped in for a cup of espresso. The place had certainly changed, but the coffee was still delicious.

We also visited my grave, which had a huge stone monument. It was strange visiting my own grave. At first I felt the man buried there was someone else. I couldn't quite identify any longer with that great composer who died nearly two hundred years ago. I felt sad, though. Then memories of my last days started flooding in and I had to walk around the back of the monument, away from George, because I was weeping.

The last place we visited was Pasqualatihaus where I lived off and on for many years.

"I've seen enough, George. I feel too emotional over seeing the places Beethoven lived and worked, and his grave. Let's go back to the hotel."

I cannot wish that things would have been different in my past life except for my poor health in later life. It was a cross to bear beyond belief. However, being without a wife and family and being deaf created a life for me out of which great music flowed. Over time it has been enjoyed by millions.

I wonder if my tenth symphony, written in a sense out of time, would eventually be heard by anyone at all.

When I returned home, I found reporters waiting for me. I found women trying to get to me. George plunged through them with me in tow up to the front door. He slammed the door on the raucous crowd.

Unfortunately, the woman who accused me of being the father of her child had set a precedent for others to accuse me. Fortunately, the DNA test I had already taken was ready to prove them wrong.

It was no secret where I lived. People drove by and stopped to look. Reporters knocked on the door. Women peered in the windows. A couple of them even found their way around the house to the patio to disturb my contemplations.

I decided to rent an isolated cabin in the woods where no one could find me. I also rented a small Steinway grand to work on. Finally I could have some peace. George found a PhD candidate in piano performance to rent my house. He was instructed to tell anyone looking for me that I would not be back for several months.

Bertha did not want to drive the narrow winding roads to my cabin, so she found employment elsewhere.

It was back to cold ham and cheese and microwaved frozen food for me. I didn't mind too much. It was worth the solitude.

Living at the cabin, I spent many a day and some nights working on my repertoire. I was so involved in my first love, playing the piano, that I neglected my tenth symphony. When I had returned to Earth my wish had been to complete a tenth symphony, but I was beginning to forget that. *Don't worry, Ludwig,* I told myself. *There will be plenty of time for writing later.*

The Steinway was quieter than my Bösendorfer, but I soon got used to it. After a while the strings seemed to have an undesirable vibration to them. The tone was also sounding muddy. I had my piano tuner come to check the piano.

"I don't hear any unusual vibration, Van. It's not your Bösendorfer, but it has a good sound." Obviously he did not have the sensitive ears that I have.

"There's a strange vibration. Don't you hear it?"

"No. I don't know what you're talking about."

"Very well. Maybe it's the damp weather. Thanks for coming over."

Even when the weather was warm and dry, the sound of the piano continued to irritate me.

George came over one day to tell me I'd been invited to play at Carnegie Hall in New York.

"I'm not ready to perform for a while. I'm enjoying my peace and quiet."

"An invitation to play at Carnegie Hall is just about the highest honor a musician can have. You can't say no, Van. You will not get another chance."

"I don't know when I'm going to get my symphony finished if I keep traipsing around the country."

"Performing at Carnegie Hall will ensure that conductors will be interested in your symphony. Otherwise, you will continue to be an unknown to them. Anyway, you've got a couple more months until the concert."

"What? You're mumbling again. What did you say?"

George repeated it a little louder, and I understood.

"Okay, I'll go. Want some coffee, a glass of wine?"

"Wine sounds good."

"Red or white?"

"Red."

George followed me into the kitchen. "Nice little hideaway you've got here, Van. Too bad your other house isn't private any longer."

"Yeah." I got out a bottle of pinot noir and a couple of glasses. I still wasn't very good at opening wine bottles. I didn't want to fumble around with an audience. "How about opening it, George? My hand hurts from writing too much."

"No problem." He opened it easily and poured some into the two glasses. We went back to the living room.

I said, "I've been wondering about these DNA tests. It's not possible, is it, to do a test on a dead person?"

"Well, yes, it is sometimes." He laughed. "What are you thinking?"

"A silly notion, I suppose, but I was wondering if one had been done for Beethoven."

"I think they did one on his hair. What do you want to know for?"

"Curiosity is all. Is there a way to get a copy of the test?"

George shook his head. "I don't know. Why are you bothering with this? Because of that hypnosis session? Think you're Beethoven?"

"No, but maybe I'm his descendant. Then maybe people would see I inherited his musical talent, maybe even his memories and wouldn't be thinking I'm crazy."

"Van, I know there's been a lot speculation about this, but you can't compare your DNA to Beethoven's. It's not available to the public. I'm not even sure they were able to get his complete DNA." George paused to take a sip of his wine. "Even if you could, some critics would say, 'So what! He's just trying to ride on Beethoven's coattails.' Bad publicity. Don't even try it." He drank some more wine.

"Like I told you before, Van, let the people wonder. There are believers and nonbelievers. It's a good balance. You don't want to upset the apple cart."

༄

The fact that I had a DNA test is public knowledge. What if someone publicity nut like the person who revealed my hypnosis session is able to get my new DNA results from my private medical records and compares it with the old? I pray it won't happen. The apple cart, as George says, will surely be upset.

The only person I would really want to know my DNA matched Beethoven was Melanie. If she knew the truth, maybe she would come back to me. Or not. She has a strong desire for children. I cannot sire children, according to Mozart. Maybe Mozart was wrong! Maybe I will just see if a doctor can tell me if I can sire children.

The answer from the doctor is no, I cannot sire children.

26

I gave a few concerts in smaller cities while I awaited my Carnegie Hall debut. None of the pianos were any good. They all had strange vibrations. You would think they would have better pianos.

I tried to work on my symphony but the crickets were getting so loud that even with the windows closed they distracted me. When they weren't chirping, I could hear a low hum like that of a truck motor running some distance away.

Hoping I could play my Bösendorfer, I paid a visit to my tenant. "Hello, Robert, how are you doing?"

"I'm great, Van. Packing up my things. I've finished my PhD and I'm off to New York."

"What did you say?"

"I said I'm packing. I've finished my PhD and I'm off to New York. I have to catch a plane. You could go through now and check the premises so I can get my deposit back."

"I didn't know you were leaving."

Robert put a stack of music into a cardboard box. "I sent the notice to your manager."

"Well, good luck to you."

"Thanks."

I went through the house and checked everything. It was clean and undamaged. "I just need to check the piano before you go."

"It's a great instrument."

I started to play it. *Oh my God! It has the same vibration as so many other pianos.* "Haven't you kept it in tune?"

"Of course I have. Your playing is amazing."

"Well I think there's something wrong with it."

"There's nothing wrong with it."

Perhaps he does not have the sensitive hearing I do. "Well, never mind. You can have your full deposit back, but I didn't bring a check. Can I send it to you in New York?"

"That's fine." He gave me his phone number and his address in New York so I could send him his rental deposit.

～

We arrived early at Carnegie Hall. George and I were in my dressing room. He warned me, "I know you want a perfect piano, but this time, no matter what you think, I don't want you to say anything about the piano here or try to fix it. It would be an insult to the Institute and to the audience. Just work with it, however it is. It's probably one of the best concert pianos in the world."

"You don't know what it's like to have my musical sensitivity and to have to play a bad piano. I'll try, George. Anyway, as you say, the piano is probably one of the best. I'll go check it now." I went out onto the stage and sat down at the piano. *Why am I hearing those crickets? How can there be crickets here?* It was then I realized I was losing my hearing. Not quite the same as in my previous life, but losing it nevertheless. I played a little on the piano. The strange vibration was there, only it wasn't in the piano, it was in my ears. There was no way I could perform now, or ever.

I went back to the dressing room and cried.

"What's wrong?"

"I'm losing my hearing, that's what! I can't play. It sounds terrible to me."

"You have to play! It's too late for them to get someone else."

I fished out the phone number of my ex-tenant. "He's here in New York. He's a young virtuoso. Ask *him* to play if you want. He's good." I didn't know how good he was but he was my only suggestion. I left before George could say anything more. I took a cab back to the hotel. It was the biggest fiasco of my short career in this century. Who else had ever canceled Carnegie Hall at the last minute?

Needless to say, after the dismal flight home, that was the last time I saw George. I thought he had become my friend, but he dropped me like a hot potato. I felt so low, I would have dropped me too if I weren't me.

It didn't take long for reporters to start knocking at my door. I didn't answer the door. When night fell and they had gone, I drove to my cabin and stayed there for a couple of weeks. I have nothing to do now but work on my symphony. A lot of good Mozart's valise had done for me. Ha! It was a big joke after all. Why did he do it?

I'm not writing Melanie any more letters. She didn't want me when I could hear. She'd want me even less now.

I like my little cabin in the woods, and spend most of my time there, but I have come back to my house today to check on it and soak in the bath. The cabin only has a shower.

My hearing is getting worse. Now I hear uncontrolled, dismal organ or orchestral music. It's interfering with my symphony writing. I can't hear my symphony over it. It is driving me crazy. My dream has deteriorated into a nightmare! That damned Mozart and his stupid valise did this! I can't stand it any more. I'm going to open it! Maybe that will stop it ruining my life!

Melanie Aliona's Notes

*T*hat was Van's last entry in his journal. I went to see him after deciding I couldn't bear to marry Nick, children or no children. Van was constantly on my mind. Every time I played the piano, I felt his presence. He had somehow wormed his way into my very soul.

I knocked on his door. There was no answer. The door was unlocked, so I let myself in. "Van? Hello!" No answer. The first thing I saw when I entered the house was the open briefcase lying on the floor. It was empty except for the words inscribed inside, "This is a dream," supposedly signed by Mozart. One side was bent in. It was dented in a couple of places on the outside. The wall next to it was dented, the entryway mirror was cracked. Apparently Van had a fit of anger and took it out on the briefcase.

I called out to him, but no answer. I went further into the house. Remnants of charred music scores rested in the fireplace, the ashes cold. *What has happened!* I looked all over the house. I went out to the garage. His car was there. *Where is he? Maybe he went for a walk. I'll wait awhile and see if he turns up.*

I was excited at the prospect of surprising him, but worried that he wouldn't come back. Did the valise really control his life here? Did he disappear after trashing it? Surely not! I never believed he was Beethoven. I thought he torturously walked the fine line between genius and insanity, and this thought only made me love him more.

I wandered around the house while I waited. The kitchen—not much to eat there. *Where is Bertha?* The bathroom—a few clothes and towels on the floor, a dirty bathtub. His bedroom—I couldn't help looking in the closets and the bed covers for signs a woman had been here—nothing. I felt relieved. The den—a notebook on the table. I opened it. *My 21st Century Life, L. V. Beethoven.* "What is *this?*" Maybe he did have multiple-personality disorder after all. I was compelled to read it. There was no way I could resist. I started reading.

It was one in the morning by the time I finished. His last written entry was that he was going to open the valise. My mind was churning, *Is it true? Is he Beethoven? No, couldn't be. Just a fantastic delusion.*

It was too late to go home. I slept in his bed. The next morning I looked through his scores in the music room. No sign of his symphony. Did he burn it? Were those its ashes in the fireplace? I went home. Every day for the next week I went back to his house. Everything was exactly as I had left it. I couldn't help but think perhaps he had left this earth when he opened that valise. I checked his bank account online. Bills were still being paid automatically, no ATM withdrawals or charges since before I first went to his house.

I filed a missing person's report. Sheriff's deputies scoured the area but found nothing.

What was to be done with his property? I looked through his papers for some mention of family, or even a will. I found a will. He left everything to me, "My Immortal Beloved, Melanie Aliona." I was deluged with tears of grief.

I contacted a lawyer. Since no body was found, Van could not be declared dead for seven years. I was appointed conservator until he was found or until the seven years were up.

He had wanted people to read his journal. I wanted to honor his wish by getting it published. I stayed in his house in the guest room while I typed his journal into my laptop. His spirit seemed to comfort me in my sorrowful task. At times I felt his presence in the house.

One evening I was playing his "Theme for Melanie," a piano reduction of the symphonic movement. I felt his presence so strongly that I stopped and looked out into the entry. He was standing there, smiling. *His ghost!*

"That was beautiful, my dear Melanie. I couldn't have played it better."

The ghost was speaking!

"I . . . I . . . thought you were dead. Are you a ghost?"

He laughed and approached me. "I have felt like one these past weeks, but now that you're here I feel more alive than ever!"

He took me in his arms and kissed me passionately, then he let go of me. "Are you just visiting, Melanie, or are you here to stay?"

"Here to stay if you'll have me."

"What about Nick, children?"

"I couldn't forget you. You were constantly on my mind. I couldn't stand being with Nick any longer. That's over."

He took me in his arms again and kissed me.

"What have you been doing here?"

"I was typing up your amazing journal, hoping to get it published."

"Well, go right ahead. I'm losing my hearing, can't play any more. The piano sounds terrible to me when I play. There's nothing more I want to write except for my symphony. You can say in my journal that you're here with me and we're living happily ever after. I hope you can get it published, maybe even made into a movie."

"I don't know about the movie part, but I'll try."

"I'm glad I smashed Mozart's valise. That 'quantum field' of his has no more hold over me. Now that you're here, my life is almost perfect."

We made our way to the bedroom to start our "happily ever after" life.

⌒

"I'm so happy sitting here having breakfast with you, my love. It's a dream come true. And, I love these waffles." He drenched them with some more syrup.

I smiled as I added half-and-half and sugar to the too-strong coffee he had brewed from espresso beans.

"Don't you like my coffee?"

"It's delicious—with cream and sugar."

"So you aren't happy with my coffee. Are you happy with the rest of me?"

"I'm very happy, Beethoven. I thought you were dead. I didn't realize how much I hurt you until I read your journal. You have been through so much, and now you're losing your hearing."

"I can bear it with you by my side. But what about your wish for children?"

"We could adopt, but I'm not sure an adoption agency would approve you after all the publicity. Then there's artificial insemination from a sperm donor."

"What is that?"

"A doctor would inject me with an anonymous donor's sperm collected at a clinic—the way you had your sperm count tested."

"Not sure I would like that, but give me some time to get used to the idea." He took my hand. "I would love to have a family, especially with you."

"I'm not in a hurry."

After breakfast Van cleared the table, while I loaded the dishwasher.

"Will you live here with me? There's plenty of room. I spend a lot of time at the cabin so I wouldn't get in your way. When I finish my symphony, we could get married."

"I would love to live with you. I'd like a little time to think about the marriage part."

He put his arms around me and kissed me tenderly. "Okay, but don't think too long. I can hardly wait for us to be wedded."

∽

I moved in with him. I had rented a furnished apartment, so I didn't have much to bring. It worked out well for us that Van had the cabin. He would walk over there in the mornings. He could work there undisturbed while I worked on my Master's Thesis and played the piano.

I took him to the ear doctor. He has cochlear otosclerosis. Surgery or medication might help. Van agreed to try the medication. He won't even consider an operation until he finishes his symphony, which is nearly complete. He was fitted with a hearing aid which he said makes things sound louder but not very clear. Strangely, it is thought that Beethoven suffered the same disease.

Van also has musical ear syndrome, which causes him much irritation when he is trying to compose. He hears poorly composed music he cannot control. It has made him difficult to live with at times. Fortunately he can get away to his cabin. I have to call him there often to remind him to quit working so hard and come home.

⌒

On one occasion Van was at his cabin for three days and nights straight before he came home. When he finally showed up, he set a fat music score on the piano and said, *"Voila! C'est fini!"*

"You've finished it?"

"Yes, my dear." Humming a waltz, he danced me around the room. "Would you like to hear it?"

"Of course I would. Do you think we can get an orchestra to play it?"

"I can play some of the themes for you now." He sat down at the piano.

"But your hearing, Van. You said you couldn't play any more."

"I can play well enough, just not well enough for the public. I can't be sure the tones will be perfect. It would be nerve-wracking for me. I know you can understand any imperfections. I will listen with my mind. I want you to hear what I have done."

"Do you mind if I record it?"

"Go ahead if you like."

I set up a mike that had been standing in a corner of the room and never used. I hooked it up to my notebook. "I'm ready when you are."

He played for an hour straight. It was amazing!

"Bravo! Encore, Van, please. One more!"

"Just one more, Melanie. This is a song I wrote for you and about you."

When he was finished, he joined me on the couch. I was crying.

He put his arm around me. "What's the matter, my love?"

"That was so sweet."

"Well, dry your tears and let's have some dinner. I'm famished."

"You must be hungry for real food after being holed up for three days with only a microwave. Can I fix you some pasta with ham and walnuts and parmesan?"

"I love it! I'll dig out the best red wine and we'll celebrate!"

During dinner we discussed the possibilities for his symphony. Send it around to conductors or pay an orchestra to perform and record it.

As we talked, his excitement waned. He turned almost melancholy. "Enough talk, my love. Let's take our wine to the bedroom."

After our lovemaking he got up from the bed. He said, "I must take a walk. Something is calling me." He started getting dressed.

"Do you want me to go with you?"

"No, I must go alone, but I will see you in my dreams."

"What?" I sat up.

He seemed full of sorrow. "I . . . mean you are with me always, even when you are not by my side. Don't worry. We will be together eternally." He kissed me lightly and went out into the hall.

Something was wrong, I didn't know what. I put on my bathrobe and went out after him. He was already out the door. He was walking down to the road, the briefcase in his hand! I hurried out the door to catch up with him. Before I could get down the steps I saw him disappear into the trees. I didn't know which way he had gone, so I went back in the house.

I was worried about him, but I figured he was headed for his cabin, perhaps to spend some time in solitude with his thoughts, whatever they may be. I went into the music room. I looked at the stack of his magnificent tenth symphony. I picked up the first page and saw the opening measures, then the notes started to disappear! The paper disappeared. The whole manuscript disappeared. Everything—the piano, the furniture, walls—began to fade away until only my personal belongings remained, lying in the grass. I was standing in a meadow where the house had been. Even his journal was gone.

Tears streaming, my hands shaking, I gathered up my things and stuffed them in my car as fast as I could. I got a room at a hotel and cried myself to sleep.

The next morning I checked my notebook to see if my typed copy of his journal was still there. It was! And the recording as well! These are all I have left of him, Ludwig van Beethoven, the greatest composer of the twenty-first century. He said his wish was to write his tenth symphony, and that he did. If only he had also wished to have it performed by an orchestra, his manuscript might still be here. *He* might still be here.

C'est fini.

C. C. Vaughan studied classical piano for many years and majored in music at Sonoma State University. Born in Pawhuska, Oklahoma, she and her family moved to Bartlesville, Oklahoma, when she was six years old. She attended Oklahoma State University, then moved to San Francisco.

She was a Senior Editor for a small publisher, and is now a freelance editor and publishing coordinator for self-published authors.

Vaughan and her husband, composer pianist Robert Ellis live in Sonoma County, California. Her son and her daughter-in-law live in San Diego, California.